I'm

Back!

J.S. Morton

Dystopic

*First published in the UK in 2025
by Dystopic Publishing Ltd
71-75 Shelton
Street Covent
Garden WC2H
9JQ
ISBN 978-1-7395495-3-4*

*www.facebook.com/dystopicpublishing
www.instagram.com/dystopicpublishing*

ONE.

I'm alive!

No thanks to June—fucking June.

Fucking Mike.

My nosy neighbour's husband just had to die—sending his wife into a grief spiral—one which culminated in her almost shooting my leg off with a sawn-off shotgun. Then I fell into the water at Southampton docks!

But I survived.

I woke up in a French hospital weeks later with not a clue what was going on—oo-la-laa.

And then, since I was missing and presumed dead, I decided to stay that way.

June went to prison—of course—but that's what you get WHEN YOU SHOOT SOMEONE (at close range) WITH A FUCKING SHOTGUN.

But all that is in the past. Wayyyyy (twenty-five-ish years) in the past. I know I had a life, a lover, friends, family, and a daughter on the way. But I'm a serial killer. I figured, who needs one of them in their life? It's like one of those dickheads that decides to keep a pet wolf! Wolves belong in the wild.

And serial murderers. Well, they don't really belong anywhere (I guess some would argue Hell), but if there's one place they should be, it's in isolation.

And, I know, I know. I only kill bad people. Unless you're a cunty little lawyer that spoke to me (rudely) in the men's room at a party. But that nearly got me in trouble. I have learned since then. And I have been staying out of the fucking way. I've found that the less I mix with people in general, the less I feel the urge to strangle them.

It's been six months and twenty-five years since I last took a life, and I am trying to keep it that way.

Since I woke up on the continent (I have no idea how I got there, but, hey, Darryl from *The Walking Dead* managed to float his way from America to Paris), I decided to move further south. I rented a small cabin in the woods (nothing like the film) in a remote part of the French Alps.

I had money tucked away (my wife had been a wealthy lawyer), and being a killer, I had running away money stashed away—just in case. And since then, well, I've been reading and hunting—lots of fucking hunting. Far too much hunting. Way, way too much hunting. But detoxing from killing was always going to involve baby steps and substitutions. So what if I've almost depopulated an entire region? I haven't killed any humans . . . and that's a good thing, right?

But I do feel the occasional pang of guilt about how I left. *What? I'm a murderer, so I shouldn't' feel?*

I'm a sociopath. We process these things differently.

I had a girlfriend named Ophelia, who I left quite literally holding the baby. I left my friends Abdul, Maureen, Rich Richard, and Cautious Cathy all dealing with grief. And I left my parents and my sister Judy to bury the non-existent corpse of their son/brother.

So, I feel kind of shitty about that. But on the flip side, most of them were unwittingly aiding and abetting one of the UK's most notorious serial killers.

It's all about balance.

And my daughter. My baby girl (whose hand I've never held) will be approaching her twenty-sixth birthday by now). Okay, so leaving was shitty. But you see my problem? They were better off without me.

As for myself and my asylum, well, things are good. I'm bored and lonely, and I'm endangering species left, right, and centre. And my patchwork quilt of a leg has healed as much as it can. It hurts in the cold. And I live in the French-fucking-Alps, and it's constantly fucking freezing. Who even thought, 'Oh, let's build huts from wood and place them in the coldest spots on Earth?'

It couldn't be much colder unless it were made from jelly. And I have a fireplace. I do. But my house is made of wood. The fire is surrounded by its juicy fuel, and I constantly fear burning the place down.

But that is not the point. I am alive, as are a good many other people since I moved into semi-isolation. And my friends and family have one less murderer in their life . . .

. . . But I do occasionally have to venture into town. And, as it turns out, France wasn't exactly the best place for me to move to when it comes to people.

No offence to the French. It is a beautiful country with a LOT of culture. But part of that culture is révolution and 'we don't give a fuck', which is bad for a serial killer with a short fuse who doesn't care much for bad manners.

And I don't speak a word of French. I've tried. But I'm British. We don't learn other languages—it's not in our DNA.

And today is one of those days.

Venture into town I must . . .

Town is a word I use rather loosely.

There are craters on the moon that are more densely populated—probably with more amenities.

It is no West Quay shopping centre.

But it has a post office, a pharmacy, a baker, a butcher, and, sadly, no candlestick maker. It has five cafes and several local bars—none of which I'm welcome in.

Après Ski is a theme. And there is also a small supermarket that sells most things I need. I have no idea what the opening times are or if there are set opening times. So, I usually venture into town just after lunch, and most of the time, things are open.

I pull up outside 'The Marché' in my old, beaten-up Mitsubishi Pajero and kill the engine. It is March, and although it is still freezing and covered in snow, most tourists have long since departed.

Tourists are a temptation.

I throw my hat over my head, crack the door open and brace for the icy blast that is about to pervade my entire body.

I have my gloves on by the time I am out of the car, but they do little to stop me from feeling like I am facing the elements stark-bollock-naked. I shuffle my way quickly into the shop, and I nod (politely) to the old French lady who is sitting at the till. Her disinterest peaks as I arrive, and she immediately returns to filing her nails. I wander around the old supermarket, filling my basket with the essentials. Surprisingly, I don't have much need for meat. But I do need all the other things that are required to sustain a human body, and I would (quite literally) kill for some Marmite and some Earl Grey, but these things are not readily found in small French supermarkets—death or not.

The custom in the shop is sparse, and I make my rounds unmolested before dumping my items down on the till. The woman looks up from her nails. Then across at me and then back to her nails. She waits until I have finished unloading my items until she deigns to stop filing, and I am forced to clear my throat to jolt her into action. It might be quicker if I killed her. But then I'd be forced to scan my own items, and I don't fucking work here. She is small, she is frail, and she is French. She knows I am the English man from the hut who speaks no French, and she begins to scan my items at a snail's pace.

I fall into my head as the items scan away on the old till, and before I know it, my goods are on the other side of the conveyor, and she is back, filing away at her nails.

How much filing do they even need? What is she, a werewolf?

With my attention back in the room, she says nothing, moves one of her excessively filed nails up to the screen, and points at the price.

Or at least that's what I saw in my periphery—my focus was elsewhere. Because next to the till is a small collection of Newspapers—99.9% of which are French—we are in France. But because this place does see seasonal skiers. They do have the odd English newspaper, and I can't quite take my eyes off of this one . . .

. . . . I can't take my eyes off it because the front page of this particular rag has a headline that halts me in my tracks.

The headline reads:

'More bodies attributed to the Hampshire Hacker'.

And I remain frozen. Because next to the headline is a picture of a young woman. And I don't know who she is, but at the same time, I know exactly who she is.

I don't know what cruel twist of fate transpired to make this happen. But she has my eyes, crooked smile, and even bent nose. It's as though someone took a picture of me, ran it through one of those face apps, and decided to change my fucking age and gender.

I lurch forward toward the paper and pick it up from the shelf. And I read the caption:

'Task force leader finds more bodies linked to the Hampshire Hacker—refuses to comment.'

That's my girl!

Quite literally.

That is my girl. And it would seem that through some weird shift of destiny, she is very much looking for me, and she doesn't even know it yet.

At this point, I should probably add that my trail of destruction, in England, has been somewhat uncovered. I have no idea how they have linked the corpses together, but it would seem that my 'carefully disposed of bodies' might not have been all that carefully disposed of. No one knows it is me . . . yet. But I am a wanted man in the UK.

I am the Hampshire Hacker—Newspapers! Never very inventive!

I hear some angry words in French along with the word 'Bibliothèque', and I turn to see the lady glaring at me, still tapping at a price on the screen. I set the paper down on the conveyor and she sighs, picks it up, scans it and then returns to pointing at the price screen.

I pay up, gather my belongings and scamper back to my car. I dump my shopping on the passenger seat and stare hard into the eyes of the girl in the paper. My girl!

When I moved, I decided to avoid temptation altogether, and as much as I could (and probably should) have looked up my daughter, lover, friends, and family, I haven't.

But I am in no doubt that this is my daughter. And even if she doesn't know it, she is looking for her dad.

And a girl needs her father.

She's calling out to me.

It is not a sensible choice. But it's the only one I have.

It looks like I'm going back to England. . . .

TWO.

The problem with going back to England is that I didn't leave. Not properly, anyway. Not according to His Majesty's Customs. I got shot and ended up on a boat, and I presume they thought I was an asylum seeker, so they shipped me back to France—helpful. I woke up in a French clinic. I healed, escaped, and then hitched my way south.

And since I am missing and presumed dead, trying to prove who I am in some small government office in the South of France just isn't going to cut it.

There is only one person I know who can easily get me back into my God-forsaken-country:

Judy!

Judy. My pain in the backside antithesis of a sister, Judy.

It turned out we were more alike than I thought and that Judy, too, had more layers to her—like an onion.

But I fucking hate onions. After twenty-five years in absentia, appealing to my sister's better nature will be like taking a nail clipper to a testicle.

But appeal I must.

As much as I've semi-enjoyed being on ice. It's time for me to get back to my life.

My daughter is looking for me. I'm no Sigmund Freud—clearly—but I'd say there's something in that.

Daughter searches for her dad.

It's adorable.

Okay, she is searching for a sociopathic killer. She doesn't know that. But she is looking for me.

I have to do something about that, so I put the car in reverse and start the long journey home.

I get home, step from the car, slip, grab my belongings from 'The Marché', and blunder up the path to my hut.

The cold is one of the many things I'll not miss about this place. But it has been fucking beautiful.

The log cabin greets me like an incoming strain of norovirus, and I step inside, it is fractionally warmer in here—fractionally.

Once inside, I store my shopping—that I won't be needing—and set about rummaging about in a box under my bed.

When I came to in *that French clinic,* I had little left on me. But I did have a list of phone numbers that I kept on me— just in case.

And I still have that list, which is good because Judy's phone number is on there. It's been twenty-five years, but I know Judy. It will be the same number.

I stand from the floor and raise my ageing frame to the bed. Once there, I grab one of my burner phones from the bedside table and dial the eleven numbers (plus the dialling code) that I never thought I'd have to dial again.

Judy!

I type the numbers in. I dial. I wait.

The phone rings:

'Hullo!'

'Hello, Judy. It's me,' I say.

'Me, who?' asks Judy.

'Oh, come on, Judy. You know it's me.'

'Brother mine, I presume?'

I nod.

'Yes, Jude.'

'What do you want, Arthur?'

'What, no questions? No "Thank God you're alive, Arthur?"'

'Oh, thank God you're alive, Arthur. Happy?'

'Yes.'

I am confounded.

You see, my sister, Judy, and I haven't always seen eye to eye—we've never seen eye to eye. She is my nemesis. But she does know the real me, and there was one very telling time when she came for me when no one else could.

In a former life, I stabbed a lairy lawyer named Theo in the eye at a well-attended party. Theo's body reappeared, and I almost found myself in big trouble. Come to think of it, bodies are reappearing now.

That's not the point.

Judy came through for me.

And I'm hoping she'll come through for me again.

I thought Judy was merely a gossip/advice columnist for a magazine. But she is much more than that. She is the woman with the dirt, so she can get almost anything she wants done.

'I'm not clearing up your mess. Not this time, Arthur. It's gone too far.'

'Can you get me back in the country?'

'Of course, I can get you back in the country. I can have you picked up in an hour. But you left, Arthur. You should stay gone.'

'Do it! My daughter. She needs me.'

'She is looking for you. That's true. But, Arthur, not in a way that you'll like.'

'Regardless, I need to come back for her.'

'Arthur, there is something you should know.'

'What?'

'It's Ophelia.'

I shuffle on my bed for comfort, press the phone against my ear with my shoulder, and rub my hands together for warmth.

'What about her?' I ask.

'She's dead, Arthur?'

'Dead?'

'Yes, Arthur. It's something you are quite familiar with—'

'But how?'

'She had a heart attack, Arthur.'

'But—but.' I genuinely don't know what to say.

In one generation of my life, there was Melissa. And Melissa was my first love. When she died, I was anxious and depressed for a long time. I wallowed in my excessive self-pity, and I couldn't bring myself to do anything—not even to kill.

But then I met Ophelia, and the darkness moved out of my brain. I realised that there could be more than one person who accepted me for who I am: warts, killings, and all.

But now that Ophelia has gone, I feel the icy cold of loneliness circling me. For as long as she existed, I was known through and through. But without her, no one knows my true identity. Not my real self. I am Holmes without Watson. Bruce Wayne without Alfred. Or Dom Toretto without a car. I am lost, adrift, and my fucking God, I have to find my daughter.

'Arthur, hullo, Arthur.'

'Yes, Judy,' I say.

'Dammit, Arthur, don't you feel anything at all?'

I pause. I sigh. I remember that I need Judy's help.

'Can you get me back to England or not?'

'Of course. Arthur, help is on the way. Sit back, relax, and I'll have someone pick you up within an hour. But you are a wanted man here, Arthur. Coming back opens a massive can of worms. I presume you have heard about your daughter and what she does?'

'I've heard. Wait—Judy, how do you know where I am?'

'Oh, Arthur, did you think I hadn't found you?'

'And you didn't think to reach out?'

'Where would be the fun in that? Plus, you know, the phone works both ways.'

'I do—but you—you knew I was alive?'

'Yes, Arthur.'

'And you—'

'Look, Arthur. You departed, and you left everyone here holding the bag. Not to mention clearing up your mess. I know that feelings might not come readily to you. But the rest of us do at least feel something. Mum, Dad, your friends. They have been dealing with you being gone. And I have had to keep this a secret all this time, Arthur. So, no. You don't get to lecture me. If you want to run off and hide, that's your business.'

'But you will help me?'

'I will. But this is tricky business, Arthur. Bringing Arthur Norman back from the dead will take some explaining.'

'Judy, can't you make me someone else?'

'I can, and please remember we are talking on a mobile phone. But if you want to be there for your daughter, you need to be her father. So, we are going to have to resurrect Arthur Norman. Which is going to take some explaining.'

'Explaining—' I don't even get to finish my sentence before Judy cuts me off.

'Yes, Arthur. You've been missing and presumed dead for nearly twenty-six years. This isn't an elaborate work of fiction. This is real life. You can't just disappear for almost three decades and then waltz back into people's lives.'

I shuffle on the bed and lie back down so my head faces the wooden ceiling. I like the logs, but I wish they emitted heat.

'So, you have a plan?' I ask.

'I know a few doctors, Arthur. I'm sure we can have some of them say you've been suffering from amnesia until now.'

'And that's the master plan, is it?'

'Well, it's that, or we tell everyone that you've been hiding out in a cabin for twenty-six years while an innocent woman sits in jail.'

'June?' Fucking June.

'Yes, Arthur. She was sent to jail for your murder. You've literally ruined lives.'

'She did shoot me,' I add.

'Arthur?'

'Fine, we'll go with amnesia.'

'Okay, good. Get your story straight. And I'll act like I'm pleasantly surprised to see you.'

'Can you manage that?'

'Very droll, Arthur. Pack your shit up. I'll have a car drive you to the nearest Airport. Someone will meet you there with a passport.'

'Judy?'

'Yes, Arthur.'

'I'm almost out of money.'

'Well, you'll have to get a job then, won't you?'

'Very good, Judy.'

'I'll see what I can do, Arthur. I have to go. Be ready in an hour.'

'Oh, Jude, Jude.'

'Yes, Arthur,' she replies with an annoyed strain in her voice.

'What happened to the house?'

'Well, you left everything to Ophelia. And she, in turn, left it all to your daughter.'

'And the Alfa?'

'Arthur?'

'What? It will be a classic by now.'

'I believe it's in the garage.' I pump my fists on the bed, then slide back into my head.

'When did it happen?'

'Ophelia?'

'Yes.'

'About a year ago.'

A small tear forms and trickles its way from my eye socket. It rolls down my cheek and lands with a sploosh on my neck.

'Arthur?'

'I'll see you soon, Judy.'

And with that, I hang up.

When I met Ophelia, I was a raggedy mess. I was too scared to leave the house, afraid of killing the local cat killer and wallowing in excessive self-pity. Ophelia found me. She saw me, and she saved me. There are many people whose passing does not bother me (I've caused a fair few myself), but Ophelia's departure does rock me. She deserved better than I gave her, and I hope she was happy in the end.

Still, there is no sense in dwelling on bad news. I have a flight to catch and a daughter to find.

I stand from the bed, stretch, and begin to pack up my meagre belongings. I hope that Judy has got me hold baggage . . .

The closest airport to me (of any relevance) is in Lyon. As promised, Judy has a car at my door within the hour. The dour French driver arrives, stops, and remains seated in the car.

So, I assume he's here for me. I am ready to go by the time the car arrives, and I trudge outside carrying what little I have.

I open the door and get in. He turns about, looks me up and down, grunts, and then returns to his duties. He is difficult to describe: tall, dark, gaunt, at a pass handsome and very laconic. But I am not here for the conversation. He puts the car in gear and sets off. I stare out the rear window as I watch my hut disappear in the distance and wonder what adventures will await me when I return to the United Kingdom.

THREE.

My flight was bumpy. It would be safe to say that I'm not the biggest fan of flying. Filling a hollow metal tube full of people and baggage and then getting up to horrendous speeds to get it off the ground to cruise through the air at hundreds of miles an hour seems a tad unrealistic.

Not to mention that, but you are literally crammed into a small area of the world's most unbearable people. It doesn't seem to matter what flight you are on; you find yourself surrounded by the worst of humanity.

People who kick the back of seats. People who stand up the minute the plane lands. People who demand drink after drink and then require endless trips to the toilet even though they have a window seat. Screaming babies, angry parents. And then there are the general dickheads. And. And, if you are fortunate, you run into a bunch of football louts or stag do bellends dressed in offensive t-shirts.

And although it has been nearly twenty-six years since I last took a life. I almost took a dozen on the plane.

But land we did, safely, and having breezed (because I am a British citizen, and therefore subjected to no scrutiny at all) through Customs—with my new passport, I arrive, in arrivals, to a familiar sight. One that fills me with both hope and dread.

JUDY!

'Arthur,' is the first thing she says to me as I trundle through the airport towards her. I arrive just short of her feet. We embrace in a manner that reminds me of taking a sander to my entire body, and when she finally releases me, she says: 'You got old!'

'Thanks, Judy,' is my reply. She, too, looks much older but, at the same time, the exact same. Her blonde hair is greying at the edges, and she has wizened and shrunk. But she is still unmistakably a 'Norman', and as I look at her crooked smile and bent nose, I am forced to confront the image of my daughter once more.

I shake away the notions of my offspring, and I follow Judy towards the exit.

'Come along, Arthur,' she says. 'We don't have all day.'

It's weird because it has been twenty-five and a bit years since I last saw my sister, but it could have been yesterday. I am excited to be back in my home country and even more excited to be out of the cold. I will miss the scenery. But as my body temperature starts to rise, I can feel a certain blood lust rising with it. A man walks by me, and his shoulder clips mine. I stop. I seethe. I picture myself stabbing him in the shoulder as retribution. *There. How do you like that, shoulder-clipping-man?*

Judy walks backwards towards me and takes me by the hand, shaking me from my revenge reverie. It's weird; it's almost like being in the cold chilled me out. And now that I'm back . . .

'Arthur,' scolds Judy. 'I'm in the short-stay car park. It's costing me a fortune as it is.'

'Judy, you have tonnes of money.'

'That is beside the point, Arthur. And I've spent enough of it on you? Have you forgotten about that pen I bought you?'

And just like that, I'm back to being tucked in the palm of Judy's fucking hand.

She is right. As she so often is. I killed RIP Theo with his gold pen. I stabbed him right in the eye with it. Then, I buried him in freshly poured concrete. But there was one slight problem. I left the pen, complete with my fingerprints, on his corpse.

Theo was found, and the pen wound up in evidence. I don't know how she did it, but she bought that pen's freedom—along with mine.

But she goes on about it. 'Ooh, I kept you out of jail, Arthur.'

But she did keep me out of jail, and now I am free to meet my daughter. Now that I am back, another tiny bit of guilt tugs at my sleeve. I did stay gone for a while. Maybe I should have returned sooner.

There is no sense dwelling, and certainly, with Judy, I don't have the time.

Before I know it, we are in her (new) BMW M3 and we are on our way out of the short-term parking at Gatwick Airport.

FOUR.

I don't know how one goes about returning from the dead, especially when I am supposed to be feigning some limited capacity.

But I can only imagine that wandering back into the lives of the people I left behind will be a shock.

Judy wired me some money—enough to get myself settled, and then, since it was early evening, she dropped me off at my friend Abdul's house.

And here I am, waiting outside—bottle of wine in hand. I have been standing here for ten minutes, and I've got inside my head. On the other side of this door stands Abdul and Maureen. My favourite couple in the whole world. My best friend, my brother, my confidant (for most things non-murder related). I have been missing and presumed dead for twenty-five years. I have no idea how a normal person goes about processing that.

But I dealt with my share of grief (which came as a surprise) when Melissa died. And I know what it's like . . . and as a fair dose of irony, I also know what it's like to have them return from the dead.

You see, my wife, Melissa, wasn't dead. She is now, though, which seems to be a common theme among the women in my life.

I knock.

I wait.

The door opens slowly.

And that's when I see him! My friend Abdul in all his hairless glory.

'Bro?' is all he says. And I nod.

He steps from the door and throws his arms around me in what is probably the warmest embrace I have ever felt.

He holds me, and we stand there—arm in arm, for what feels like an eternity.

When he finally releases me, tears are in his eyes. He places his hands on either side of my shoulders and looks me up and down.

'You got old!'

I nod.

'So did you!'

We hug once more, and then Abdul steps back into the house.

'Where have you been, Arthur? We thought you were dead.'

'So did I,' I say. 'So did I.'

He nods.

'It's a long story,' I say.

'Well, you'd better come on in then,' he says as he ushers me into the house.

Having to explain a story that you made up about how you forgot everything (even though you remember everything) is not an easy feat.

But explain I did. And now Abdul is sitting here—tears in his eyes—just watching me.

'But why did June shoot you?' he asks.

I shake my head. 'I have no idea, Abdul. But grief makes people do funny things.

He nods. 'I suppose it does.

'Where will you stay?'

'I don't know,' I say genuinely. I once had a grand house here and a house in Greece. Now my house is occupied by my daughter, whom I've never met. And fuck knows what happened to the place in Greece. Either way, Greece is a long way from where I need to be right now, which is here with my daughter.

My daughter.

'Will you stay here tonight?' Abdul asks. 'Maureen will be home at eight. I—' Abdul cuts his sentence short as he gets lost in thought. 'I don't even know how I go about telling her. Do we wait until she gets home? Do I message her, Bro-Mance, what do I do?'

I shake my head.

'Who else knows you are alive?'

'Just Judy at the moment.'

'Fucking Judy,' says Abdul.

'Tell me about it,' I say.

'I guess I'll wait until she gets home. She'll make the guest bedroom up for you, and we'll go from there.'

'Thanks, mate,' I say genuinely.

'What will you do?'

'Rent a flat, I suppose?'

Abdul nods. 'Well, you are welcome to stay here until you do.' I nod.

'You know, your daughter is living in your old house.'

'I know. I know,' I say. Yes, Abdul, I'm keenly aware that I left my daughter behind, and now she is parentless and looking for me.

Our conversation is halted by Abdul rising from the sofa and going to get another bottle of wine. It's strange, all these years in absentia, and it feels like I never left. One thing is for sure:

I'm back!

FIVE.

Maureen is a surgeon at Southampton General Hospital, and she arrived home to possibly the biggest surprise of her life! Remember your husband's friend, who regularly frequented the house, the one you thought was dead? Well! Ta-da. He's not dead.

It's safe to say it was something of a shock. But we humans are a resilient bunch, and it wasn't long before things started to look like old times.

We ate. We drank. We talked.

Then, having set the world to rights, we slept.

And now here I am, lying in bed, raring to go for my first day back! As I lie here, the thought does cross my mind that I might be supplementing my grief at having found out that the second love of my life is dead with the need to find my daughter. There is that. I might be doing that.

But she's my daughter. She is lost, alone, and I must see her.

First things first: I need to announce my arrival to the rest of the people in my life who are still alive. I also need to rent a flat, which will be rather difficult.

It's safe to say that I don't rate estate agents all that highly. They smile. They grin, and they talk the talk. But deep down, they are all just as evil as I am. I would rather take an ice bath in acid than deal with estate agents. But I have to rent a flat, and there is only one way to do that.

Estate agents.

I climb out of my reverie and the bed simultaneously and move into the en suite bathroom in Abdul's guest bedroom. My hosts are out of the house, and I step into the bathroom naked and study myself in the hefty mirror behind the sink.

I am a large man. But old age has seen me shrink somewhat. I am still handsome in a non-obvious way, and despite the myriad scars that my body is now littered with (I have been shot three times and stabbed once by a crazy Scandinavian gangster), I am still in reasonable shape for a sixty-plus-year-old. My blond hair is greying in patches, and the skin on my face gives away my age. I do, in fact, look old, but then I was sixty-three this year . . .

. . . And I'm a father, just a responsible, happy father.

But I can feel the darkness rising within me.

You see, I am fairly normal. I was just built with this deep, primordial anger. One that responds primarily to injustice. And I don't feel quite like myself until I get it out.

Which usually involves the death of some lowlife scumbag.

However. I am a father now. Not to mention that the bodies of my previous victims seem to be popping up left, right, and centre, and I have a task force (led by my daughter) frantically looking for me.

So, right now might not be the best time to kill. But when is it ever? All I do is play the hand that I was dealt. I get angry, and some little turd-sicle loses their life. It is a fair trade, and deep down, the universe knows that I am doing it a favour . . .

. . . Which will do absolutely nothing when it comes to pleading my defence. I shelve my thoughts, take one last look in the mirror, and step into the shower.

Despite turning the shower up as hot as it will go, I don't melt into the drain. Twenty-five minutes later, I am dressed and ready to go. According to Abdul, Rich Richard still lives in the same manor house he once did, which is good because

I think I still remember the way. I will wait until the evening to reintroduce my good self.

In the meantime, however, I have a date with an estate agent . . .

I had assumed that renting a flat would be easy. It is not. I thought that you would turn up, view it, like it, rent it. But it would seem that is very much not the case. It turns out you need to have employment, references, employment references, and to jump through just about every fucking hoop to convince the landlord that you are their preferred candidate . . . on paper.
But paper doesn't mean shit. For example, I am quite a nice guy . . . on paper. The reality is quite different. However, I am having a hard time proving that I am anyone on paper, but that can wait until I find a place I like.

The first three flats I viewed were dreadful. I want to be as close to my daughter as possible, but it would seem that the area she lives in (I lived in), just outside of Winchester, somewhere off the M3 motorway, is quite a pricey place to live. The first three were barely a step up from a room. On the one hand, having all of my amenities a (very small) stone's throw away from my bed is very handy. But I can't get over the feeling that paying close to £1200 a month to live in among my kitchen appliances will drive me stir-fucking-crazy. No, what I need is space. A luxury that isn't afforded to me here. So, I decided I had to search further afield.

And this brought me to Southampton! Southampton is a place I know rather well; after all, it was here that I bumped into Ophelia in the West Quay car park. It was here that the dread of being unknown was sucked from me, and I was brought out of the land of the dead and back to the light. And a fresh start might be just what I need. I have a lot of history in Winchester. There is a lot of darkness, and I need to stay away from the darkness. Many people (my daughter included) are looking for me, and I owe it to her to remain free. Incarceration after reintegration into her life would not be ideal. Neither would her finding out that the dark, disgusting creature she has been hunting is me—her father.

Unless, of course, she sees the good in what I do?

But that seems rather unlikely given what she does . . . and things got messy for Dexter and Deb. Not that I am comparing myself to Dexter . . .

My first viewing in Southampton was a success. The flat is just on the edge of town, not far from all the amenities that the city has to offer. The building is a former bank and even features an old vault—which might be handy. I liked the place, so I rented it!

I know, I know, I said renting is a hassle. And it is . . . unless you have money—which I do. If you pay upfront, no one cares who you are or what you do. And as much as I like that, it only serves to bolster what I have already said about estate agents . . .

. . . But now I have a place to reside, and when the traffic is good, it is only a twenty-five-minute journey to my old house, or more accurately, my daughter's house.

I should admit I am desperate to see her. But I need to play this cool. I don't know how one goes about un-abandoning a child, but I don't imagine it's easy—limited capacity or otherwise.

When Judy dropped me off, I managed to get her to do me one last favour—a car.

She reluctantly let me borrow one of her old ones, a BMW E90 M3. She had it shipped to my door, and it arrived at the same time as most of my belongings. With the movers moving in my brand-new furniture, I slink outside to check out my new car.

I like German cars, I do. But I prefer life to come with a bit of flair. Still, as I stare at the (now) classic German saloon, I can't help but feel a slightly weird feeling.

Gratitude!

I shake away notions of stupidity, unlock the car, and get in. The car has had a heavy valet, but it still smells faintly of Judy, so I remove a pack of battered cigarettes from my pocket, rack the chair back on its runners, and light a cigarette, taking a deep drag. I watch on as the movers continue to unload my pre-ordered furniture into my domicile, and I smile. Oh, what adventures await me this time around?

It is late evening, and I am cruising down the M3 motorway towards Rich Richard's house. Rich Richard is rich—obviously. I keep the car at a steady seventy (lest I get unwanted attention) and think about the evening to come. Rich Richard is my oldest friend. Our common ground has changed over the years, but we have always kept in touch . . . until I went missing for twenty-five years.

Will he have missed me?

I swallow my feelings as I change gears to get to the exit. The big car purrs as I do, and I wonder what is going on in my brain. Perhaps I am dealing with some form of limited capacity. Maybe all those years in the cold damaged my brain.

For most of my adolescence, I felt something that I didn't understand. It wasn't until I punched a kid in the nose—what, he was a dickhead—that I finally understood what most of the noise was about.

I was angry.

I realised that when I appeased my anger, I felt better about life. And I have been doing that ever since.

But then my wife, Melissa, died, and I fell into a brand-new spiral. Grief, anxiety, depression. All these wonderfully horrendous new feelings mixed in my brain, sending me wildly off-kilter.

And it's happening again now.

Granted, I haven't exorcised my anger in nearly three decades, but part of me wonders if I am starting to feel more human. Maybe that is what being a father does to you.

The gates open, and I drive through. I am still absent as I cruise down the long driveway and bring the car to a stop in the large turning circle in front of the house. The car idles, and the hum warms me. Reluctantly, I kill the engine and sit there, taking in the silence. A few lights go on around the property, and the occupants know someone is here.

The car door clicks smoothly shut as I step from the vehicle and make the short walk across the gravel to the enormous double door. I pause. I wait. I wonder. I can feel my heart beating in my chest, and I'm not certain it isn't about to rattle itself free in my rib cage and start bashing into my other vital organs. I breathe in. I breathe out. As I raise my hand to the door . . . it opens.

'Arthur? Arthur? Oh, my fucking God, Arthur! It's you.'

Bombshell number two came and went in a flash, and if I'm being honest, I preferred Judy's reaction to the news that I am alive. I don't enjoy being the centre of attention, and I dread the day that I am a national news feature.

But Rich Richard was extremely glad to see me, and it would seem that even Cathy had a few tears and many, many words of sentiment. It was emotional and intense, and I managed to escape as fast as I could.

But the good news is that everyone besides my parents and daughter knows I am alive. I have a flat, a car, and some money in the bank. I am free to reconnect with my daughter, and my God, I cannot get her out of my head.

I used to be good at this. I've never really worked—besides killing—but I always had someone or something to occupy my brain, be it Melissa, Ophelia, or an upcoming kill. But right now, there is one thing on my mind and one thing only.

My daughter!

My little girl is lost and alone. She doesn't know that her father exists, and I don't know what she is thinking. Is she like me? Does her mind revolve around endless loops of darkness? Does she think of me? Does she even care at all?

Does she even care at all?

***

I stir, rise from my brand-new armchair, and move into another part of the flat, where I sit at my new computer. Once settled, I turn on the machine and take to the keyboard.

The news article I read in France is posted on their webpage. The article gives me scant details about my daughter, but it does list her as serving at the police headquarters in Southampton. With little else to go on, I stand, power down the machine, grab my bag and keys, and head out.

The police headquarters in Southampton is a strange building. It is almost as though the architect was given a remit: *Make it look very new but simultaneously very old, and I also want it to encounter all the problems a new building shouldn't but an old one would.* For example, it leaks all the time, and five minutes after it was built, it looked five years old. But I guess it is iconic in a way, and I know exactly where to find it.

Five minutes later, I am pulling into the car park downstairs. Immediately, my eyes light up. In one of the spaces sits a bright red Alfa Romeo that I would recognise anywhere. She is driving my car. Maybe she does miss me after all!

SIX.

It's safe to say that I couldn't be a police officer—killings aside. Ten minutes into my wait, I got bored. I figured she would leave at the end of play, so there was no sense in sitting about all day waiting for that to happen. So I left . . .

. . . And now it is a quarter to six, and I am back staring at my old car. It still sits regally outside the police station, and my God, I am bored. And that's when I see her. My Daughter in all her glory. I watch her saunter out of the building with a colleague; they stop near the car, they chat, and then he puts his arm on her shoulder. I take a deep breath in as I picture throwing him to the floor and stomping on his hand. I blink, and the image goes away. I take another deep breath and focus on what it is I am about to do. Their chat continues, and clearly, she's had enough. I watch her gesticulate with her hand, then she waves, waves again, and before long, he is departing, and she is getting into her (my) car. The man she was talking to gets into his vehicle and promptly disappears. I watch her sit in the car and slump her long blonde hair back against the leather headrest. She closes her eyes and sighs.

It's now or never, Arthur. I take more deep breaths, pull myself together and exit the vehicle. It is a short walk across the road to the police station. But it feels much longer. I watch her as she remains motionless, and she looms larger and larger as I near. The engine starts as I arrive, but I am in her way. I listen to the twin-turbocharged V6 engine as it roars to life, and I drink in the requiem. I would wonder how she is affording to run such a vehicle on a police salary, but she has all of my (Ophelia's/Melissa's) money. I hear a gear engage, and I step to the side and draw what feels like my final breath. Then, I knock on the window.

And now I am face-to-face with my daughter. Twenty-six years of growing (fatherless), and here we are, together at last. She looks at me, disengages the car from its gear, and kills the engine. Her eyes meet mine and are locked together in a wild frenzy. Neither of us knows the other, but our eyes meet, and recognition forms, and we know that we both know exactly who we are.

And then an awkward-fucking-silence ensues. Our eyes remain entwined, and a marching-fucking-band could walk by right now, and it wouldn't break our stare. Then the door opens, and I am forced to take a step back, and then it happens. She steps from the vehicle. Her arms open wide, and she throws them around my ample frame. She holds me, and I am forced to throw my mind elsewhere; being grabbed by a police officer (outside of a police station) almost puts me in a spin, and my natural response would be to do something unspeakable. But this is no ordinary police officer. This is my daughter, and suddenly, the icy cold of being alone melts away, and nothing and no one matters but the two of us. Our embrace lasts for what feels like an eternity, and then when she finally removes her arms, she steps back and leans against the car, wipes her eyes and says: 'Dad?'

Being called 'Dad' hits me like a fucking southpaw to the stomach. It sucks all of the air out of me, and I feel sick and happy at the same fucking time. All this time, I've been waiting for this moment. I've been obsessing over it—dreaming about it, and I've had so much time to come up with something witty, clever, or sentimental to say . . . and I have nothing.

Dad!

Dad!

Dad!

The words rattle about my brain as I try to process it. It's like that game where you have to try and get all the tiny ball bearings into the holes, and I'm trying, but each hole is filled with fucking cement, and the balls keep popping out. I don't know what I'm doing; I don't know if I am ready to be a dad, and I have no idea what to say!

I dig deep into my brain and search for something deep and meaningful to say.

'Olivia,' I manage.

It's like the whole world stopped. And it is just the two of us alone on a new planet. I know her. I don't know her. She is part of me, a part that is missing. But I don't know where she goes.

Olivia wipes at her eyes and composes herself.

'Olivia,' I begin again. But I still don't know where to start! *Sorry, I abandoned you for the first chunk of your life. Sorry, I'm an angry sociopathic killer who doesn't know how to feel. Sorry, I'm the man keeping you up at night.*

Sorry doesn't cut it.

And I'm still standing in silence. Olivia looks at her watch and then at me. Then, before I get the chance to squeak her name out of my mouth for a third time, she says: 'I've got to get going, but do you want to come over later?'

I nod. And on the inside, I am all fist-pumps. She steps towards me and hugs me (lightly) once more before recoiling into the car. The sweet sound of the Italian horses fires up, and I am in another world. She puts the car in gear, revs the engine slightly and then backs out of the space. Then, just as I think she is about to disappear forever, she winds the window down and shouts: 'You know where you are going, don't you?'

***

Okay. So, I met my daughter and said her name twice, but not much else.

But I have an invite to my old house—the house I shared with Melissa and Ophelia, both of whom are now dead. Let's hope it isn't third time lucky with the women in my life.

I climb out of the shower and my head simultaneously. My daughter also shouted a time to be there before she departed, and it is now seven p.m. I have an hour to be there and need to get ready. But I can't get over the cold, almost matter-of-fact, way she treated my arrival. Does she not care? Was she aware? Is she like me? Does she have a limited capacity to feel? Is it possible we are more alike than I thought?

I reach into my cupboard and shelve my thoughts of what might be happening. I have a chance to find out. I have the opportunity to meet my daughter. I have the chance to do something I've been aching after for some time. I get dressed, and I feel less alone. And I'm almost smiling for the first time in years by the time I have my shirt on.

What an evening tonight is going to be . . .

SEVEN.

So here I am, standing in the grounds of my old house. And I'm stuck again. I realise that I am about to re-integrate myself into the life of my daughter, and I've yet to tell my parents that I am still alive. There are so many holes in this plot that have been my life for the last three decades, and I'm about to share them with a detective—by all accounts, a good one.

Could this be a trap? Is my old house filled with armed police officers? Am I about to be ambushed in my old pad? Will my trip down memory lane be my last trip anywhere?

Stop it, Arthur!

I wrap my hands tightly around the bottle of wine and start what might be my last walk, as a free man, towards the door of my old house. To say that it is strange to be here is an understatement. I'm nervous on so many levels, but I've been dreaming of this moment for weeks now. The late winter wind whistles past my ears as I walk down the driveway, and I'm suddenly very glad that I am no longer in France. But I can feel the dark lust rising inside me, which is truly fantastic given that I am about to insert the detective who is tracking me into my life. I know nothing about her: her life, her hopes, her dreams, or even how well she is doing with this case. She could be one piece of evidence away from piecing together the Hampshire Hacker puzzle. Our reunion could be short-lived . . . and perhaps I should have stayed in the cold.

Suddenly, a light outside the house goes on, and I am illuminated. Arthur in the spotlight. And if she didn't know I was here before, she surely does now. I hear a ruffle inside the house, and before I know it, the front door is open, and I see her standing there, illuminated by the lights that surround us. She is more than I could ever have dreamed that she'd be.

She is luminous, lithe, luscious. Here in the light, she looks more like Ophelia than I imagined. Her hair is blonde, like mine, but she has taken after her mother in most other ways. She is lean and muscular and takes excellent care of herself. She is beautiful; we made some human, and suddenly, I am reminded of my lost love. I fight back the tears as I make the walk down the long drive, and I prepare myself to speak . . .

. . . So far, I have managed just the two words. Both of which have been her name. She looks at me, our eyes meet, and she smiles. The driveway seems about ten times longer than it used to, but before I know it, I am standing in the vicinity of my daughter and, in lieu of a better plan, I extend my arms and hold out the bottle of wine. She takes it, looks at it and grins.

'Well, come on in then, Dad,' she says. I relinquish the bottle of wine, smile and then step into the foyer of what used to be my house. I sure hope that words will come to me eventually. . . .

***

'How have you been?' are literally the first words to leave my mouth! *How have you been? How have you been, Arthur? Is that really the first thing you have to say to your daughter?*

I don't get time to dwell on my underwhelming opening statement before Olivia replies:

'To be honest, not that great. This case—this case is getting to me . . . Dad.'

Dad! She called me 'Dad' again!

'Oh,' I say, 'The Hacker case?'

She nods.

'All we have is a tenuous link. Just one thing links the fifteen dead bodies we've found. And I don't think we've found the last of them. Whoever this guy is is good.'

'Or girl,' I add. 'Anyway,' I continue, 'they can't be that good if the bodies are popping up!' I say both to her and myself.

'Okay. But not if they want us to find them. Hey, Dad, I'm sorry. Would you like a drink?'

I nod. I am speechless once more. *How have you been?* Plus, two renditions of 'Olivia' are all I've really managed to say so far, and suddenly, we're bonding!

My daughter ushers me to the dining table, takes my coat, and then sits me down before shuffling off toward the kitchen.

Before I know it, my daughter has reappeared with two wine glasses and the bottle that I brought. She sets the ensemble down on the table and then begins to pour.

'Don't you have questions?' I manage as she pours away nonchalantly.

'Mum told me that you would reappear when I needed you the most.'

'She did?'

Olivia nods.

'How was she . . . your mother.'

'She missed you, but she was okay.'

'So, you don't want to know?'

Olivia shakes her head. 'I'm just glad you're here now. Everyone says you're the smartest man they know. I could use you right now. It's just as mum said.'

My ego peaks as the words fall from her mouth, although, with my trail of bodies being discovered and somehow linked together, I don't feel all that smart.

'So, what links the bodies?' I ask.

'It's some righteous kill. I know. I know what you're thinking. It's tenuous at best. But it's the best we can come up with.'

'A righteous kill?'

'Yeah, Dad, the one thing that links all of the bodies together is that they all deserved what they got. Every one of them. Even that lawyer. He was sexually harassing women at his law firm. Seven women have spoken out in the years that have passed since you were accused.'

'And you don't like me for his murder?'

'Oh, come on, Dad, you were the last person to see him alive. So what? It's just lazy police work. Not to mention the fact that they lost vital evidence; we could have this bastard by now.'

I pause and ponder as I take a gigantic sip from my wine. As much as I am keen that we are bonding, I never thought that my purpose as a father would be to help my daughter catch me.

'So, what else do you have?' I ask more out of interest to myself.

'Well, based on the methods used, we believe this person is local, probably male, and works alone. I don't think we've found all the bodies yet. And the various states of decomposition have made this all the more difficult. One thing is for certain, though. This fucker is still active.'

I almost choke on my wine as I try my best to guide it down my throat smoothly. I cough, clear my throat, and then go to speak again.

'Still active?' I almost squeak.

'Yeah, we've had some recent kills. The MO seems to be the same. All bad people, all deserving in some way.'

'So, you agree with what they are doing?'

'Agree is a very strong word, Dad. I mean, yes, these are some sick people. But justice is for the justice system. Not to mention that, but we don't have the death penalty here for a reason.'

'But you said all these people were deserving?'

'The evidence suggests so, Dad. But people have the right to a trial by a jury of their peers. This is vigilante justice.'

'But they are taking bad people off the streets.'

'They?'

'A figure of speech. I mean, whoever this is.'

Olivia tops up our wine, and the room falls silent. Our eyes meet again, and we look into them longingly.

'Don't you want to know—'

'Dad, Abdul and Maureen are like family to me. I knew about your reappearance almost straight away.'

'You knew?'

Olivia nods. I raise my glass to my face to conceal any emotions that might be forming on the outside. One thing is clear: my daughter is one smart cookie. She also doesn't seem to be that easily phased by anything.

'What will you do now that you're back, Dad?'

I swallow my wine and my thoughts along with it. I place the glass back on the table and open my mouth: 'Enjoy my retirement,' I say.

'Oh, that's a point,' says Olivia. She stands, pushes her chair back from the table, and walks into another room. Then she reappears presently, holding out a cheque in my direction.

Without even looking at it, I decline. But Olivia remains steadfast, holding the cheque out.

'No arguments, Dad. Mum left this specifically for you. It was one of her bequeaths.' I take the cheque that is beginning to quiver in her hands, and I stare at the numbers on the paper.

'I believe it was from the sale of the house in Greece.'

I fold the cheque in half and put it in my pocket. One thing is for certain: I don't need money anymore.

I should make it clear: I think money is evil. It can fuck off. I kill bad people for a sort of living, and one thing I have learned is that people do unspeakable things just for money. I have never liked it, but it sure is nice to have. Plus, after my brief stint as an 'employee', I would rather not cross that line again.

'Oh,' she says as she dips into her pockets once she is seated. 'You will probably want your car back, too.' I smile. I should say no. But I do love that car.

'Don't you need it?'

She shakes her head. 'Mum left me a lot, like a lot, a lot. I only used the car because it's yours; it is terrible on fuel.

I grin. Grab the keys and slide them into my pocket. *What? Can't a slightly sociopathic killer appreciate a good car?*

I pocket the keys, and my mind, which was pleasantly distracted, folds in on itself, and suddenly, I am reminded that someone out there is being me. Someone else is adding to my bodies. I am not the only Hampshire Hacker. And it is as insidious as it is comforting—is it comforting?—to know I am not alone, that someone else out there feels just like I do. But what if they have it backwards? Do they follow the same moral code as me, or have they made mistakes? I do take some comfort in knowing that Theo was perhaps worthy of death at my hands, but it doesn't take away the fact that it was a vitriolic rage that saw him die. What if the new me is the same? Can this place be safe with another vigilante killer on the loose? Or could it be that it is safer? I am conflicted. And as much as I wasn't keen on helping my daughter catch me, I am interested in knowing what she has on the new me.

Because I need to meet him, I need to know his intentions. I may need to stop him.

'You okay, Dad?'

I realise that I have been inordinately silent and force up my best fake grin. I beam at Olivia, and she smiles back at me—the power of a smile. I wonder if hers is as empty as mine, but I now have bigger fish to fry.

'I'm fine,' I manage. 'It's just lovely to be back.' I say as I look around the house.

It's strange because it is my house, but it's not anymore. Most of the rooms are gone. The walls have been knocked in to create an open-plan living situation, and the décor has changed vividly. I didn't update it after Melissa's death, and I am pleased to see that it has, in fact, changed.

I don't get long to admire what my daughter has done to my house until she shuffles her chair around the table until it is almost at mine. I inhale, and I catch the scent of her hair as it wafts near my face—she smells so much like her mother that it forces me back twenty-odd years and suddenly, I am no longer alone. I am so deep in my reverie that I don't notice her scootch alongside me and place her head on my shoulder.

'So, will you help me, Dad?'

The word 'Dad', along with her head on my shoulder, almost threatens to restart my cold, dead heart immediately. I take another deep breath in and allow it all to sink in.

'I think after the previous debacle, we'd be able to get you in as a consultant of some kind.'

I should confess that police stations scare me. I have spent the night in one (on a murder charge), and it was a stark reminder of what is to come. Not to mention that, but they are dull, they are grey, they are brown, and they are some of the most depressing buildings you're ever likely to step foot in. It wouldn't be a stretch to say that Chernobyl has a greater atmosphere than in some British police stations. So, no! I would not particularly like to be a police consultant . . . however, this is not solely about me, not anymore. I have a daughter, and she genuinely does need me. There is someone out there doing what I do. Someone has picked up my mantle. Picked up from where I left off. But they didn't ask permission. And I didn't ask to be who I am—I'd do anything to be free of my urges. And since I don't know the intentions of this 'New Hampshire Hacker', I will help my daughter find him. Because, for all the while that he is out there, he poses a threat to her, and that I cannot have.

'I'd love nothing more,' I lie.

'Thanks,' she says, and we sit there, her head on my shoulder and quietly stare away and into space.

EIGHT.

Arthur Norman, police consultant! At your service.

Yes, it sounds weird!

Today is my first day on the job. And I am excited. Nervous but excited. It is like it's take your dad to work day. And as much as I will spend the day around people I'd rather avoid, I will also get to spend it with my daughter. And since most of these dead bodies can be attributed to me, it will behove me to be one step ahead of the investigation—I can't get much closer than being a consultant.

But I can't get over my daughter's nonchalance at meeting her dad for the first time. Still . . .

I rise from the bed at seven a.m. and stretch. Getting old isn't all that bad, aside from the general memory loss and the fact that nearly any kind of physical exertion will hurt, regardless of how well you warm up prior. But I am up, so I stretch in preparation for the day ahead.

There is just one small, niggly task that lies in front of me before I accompany my beautiful, wonderful, smart daughter to work.

My parents!

I know. I know. I said I would tell everyone about my reappearance before embarking on this new life chapter. But in my defence, my parents were a handful twenty-five years ago. And, yet, somehow, they are both still alive and well, despite being in their nineties and on a fast march towards a century on planet Earth. But alive they are, and so am I . . . and since I didn't mention it to them, Judy just had to go ahead and jump the gun.

Fucking Judy.

Judy told my parents and the rest of my extended family that I am, in fact, still alive. Then she went ahead and gave them my phone number—the temerity. But Judy always was a thorn in my side, and since Jenny's death, my father has been excessively ornery (he's usually grumpy), so Judy deemed it necessary to tell them that I am alive.

Jenny was more boring than the intermission at a school play. But she was pretty and my parents' neighbour, and they tried to set me up with her on occasion. But Jenny's purpose in life was ostensibly for my father to flirt with her . . . at every opportunity possible. She was murdered because of me, and goddammit, women in my life do seem to wind up dead. I have to put a stop to that, starting with Olivia.

Before that, however, I wait in aching anticipation for one of the most terrifying things on the planet. Scarier than global warming, a great white shark in your swimming pool, shopping on a Sunday, or a Conservative Party manifesto. I wait for a call from my mother. . . .

The phone rings.

I shudder.

I rise from the chair I had taken a seat in and amble across my open-plan living room to the phone.

'Hello,'

'Arthur?'

'Yes, Mum,'

'Arthur, is that you?'

'Again, yes, it's me, Mum.'

'Oh, Arthur. Arthur, we thought you were dead!'

'So did I, Mum. So did I.'

'Your father hasn't been very well.'

So that's it? My resurrection gets a vague bit of sentiment, and now we've changed the topic. No wonder Jesus didn't come back. I mean, he could return tomorrow, and we'd barely even notice. Although, I have somehow compared myself to Jesus . . .

'Arthur, you there?'

'Yes, Mum.'

'Pardon.'

'Yes, Mum, I'm here.'

'I said your father hasn't been very well.'

'Yes, Mum, I heard. Is he okay now?'

'Well, he's very grey and in lots of pain.'

'Has he taken any painkillers?'

'Oh, no, he says he's fine.'

'Get him to take the painkillers, Mum.'

'Arthur?'

Silence.

'It's good to hear your voice.'

I pause, and I grin. It is good to hear my voice. It is somewhat good to hear my mother's, too. The vague, fuzzy sentiment catches me in a daze, and before I know it, I'm saying something I might regret . . .

'Is he there?'

'Your father?'

No, Mum, Tom-fucking-Jones!

'Yeah, Dad, is he there?'

'I'll go and find him!'

My mother trundles off with the phone (presumably to find my father), and all I can hear are the faint scuffles of her feet as she walks. I remove the phone from my ear and look at the Casio watch on my wrist. Realistically, I have nowhere to be (can consultants be late?), but I did promise my daughter that I would meet her this morning.

'Arthur,' comes the gruff voice from the phone in my lap. I raise the phone to my ear and say the words I never thought I would say again.

'Hello, Dad. How are you doing?'

'Good, good. I see England won the cricket.'

'They did, Dad. They did.'

'Well, I'm glad you're back, Arthur. You should come down sometime. You know, we aren't getting any younger.'

I consider this request for a moment—it's true, they aren't. I'm amazed both of them are still alive and kicking. The selfish part of me had hoped that they might die not knowing that their son is a serial murderer—that would be simpler. But something—someone—is working against me. I must join forces with my daughter and find this fiend who purports to be me. I must find him, and soon. That would put the whole thing to bed.

'Arthur?'

'Yes, Dad.'

I look at my watch. It is a quarter to eight in the morning. Time flies when you are having fun. I must leave. The watch also tells me that it is Tuesday. I have spare time.

'I'll be down at the weekend, Dad. Say, Dad, I gotta go.' I pause for a moment before adding, 'Give my love to Mum.' And then, before he has the chance to say anything else, I hang up.

Stoicism always wins in my family. For twenty-five years, I was in absentia. My return? My return is greeted by a 'you should come down'. But, hey, it's better than nothing.

I raise myself from the chair, stretch and then take the twelve steps from my chair to the door. My feet slide across the smooth laminate; before I know it, I am standing with my shoes on and my keys in my hand.

Time to go to work with my daughter!

The problem, which I may have mentioned, about getting old is that everything hurts—all the time. My back hurts, my knees hurt, my shoulders hurt constantly, and I am also approaching that point where gravity starts to become a danger! That's right, gravity. Innocent old gravity might yet be the death of me. You laugh, but old people and gravity do not get on. After all I've been through. After all the lives I have taken, I cannot succumb to gravity.

Then there is my mind! It hurts even when nothing else does, and it exacerbates the pain I have elsewhere when I do. One thing I have noticed, though, is that certain people can stop the pain. Melissa stopped the pain, likewise for Ophelia. And the more time I spend around my daughter, the more I realise that she, too, stops the pain.

And so, if it's police stations that I must endure . . .

I step outside my flat and breathe in the morning air. This is Southampton, so it smells like a mixture of mechanical grinding and seagull shit. But breathe it in, I do. I stroll across the small road that passes by the side of my flat and over to the allotted area for parking opposite. I ignore my loanee BMW and head straight for MY Alfa. I unlock it using the key as the key fob doesn't work, and I get in, nestling my body into the crisp Italian leather behind me, and I close the door.

Peace.

The smell in here is weird. It smells like a youthful woman owned it, and once again, the first thing I do is rack the chair back and light up a cigarette.

With the cigarette smoke doing its best to displace any other smells that might distract me, I start the engine, extinguish my cigarette in the ashtray—because I'm not an arsehole—and I pull my chair into a comfortable sitting position. With me sitting comfortably, I put the car in reverse, manoeuvre out of the space and set off in the direction of the town. I put the car into cruise control, and I cruise along. My mind takes over again, and I realise I should probably do something about June.

June used to live next door to me, and I think June figured me out. But she was in a sleepless state of grief at the time, and just when I thought I had talked her out of it, she accidentally shot me, hence the French sojourn. But she rots in jail, rightly so. I know. I know that's rich coming from me. But she shot me in the fucking leg with a sawn-off shotgun. Luckily, she didn't blow the whole thing off.

Anyway, since I am going to deal with the police, and she isn't, technically, guilty of murder. I probably should do something. God knows the justice system won't. I shelve my thoughts as the police station looms in the distance, and I focus on the day ahead.

Arthur Norman: police consultant. At your service . . .

NINE.

My first morning on the job was interesting. Police stations make me jittery, and that was only exacerbated by my drinking of crappy coffee. Everyone who approached me was a potential threat, and I was forced to go to my happy place every time someone got near me.

But my happy place is Olivia. And she and I are in close proximity. We are sitting in her Renault Twingo as it bounces along the road. And, yes, we are currently on our way to a crime scene . . . a crime scene. A new body has been found and attributed to the Hampshire Hacker. Which is still weird because it's both me and not me . . . like the cat, only in this case, the person involved is very much dead.

'So, where are we heading?' I ask as the car lurches into fifth gear after finally reaching cruising speed on the motorway.

'Badger Farm, not that far from home.'

I pause.

I know Badger Farm. It's where Jarrod Walker lived!

Jarrod was supposed to be my first kill after my wife Melissa's death. But I fucked up. Jarrod's girlfriend came home, and I got distracted by their garage. I came back to find a police cordon and both Jarrod and his girlfriend dead. It later transpired that my late wife wasn't late, and she had been keeping tabs (and killing for) on me.

But Melissa is dead, and it's insidious that the person who has taken up my sword is also now killing in my former stomping ground.

Silence eats its way into the car as I fall into my head, and before I know it, we are pulling up at the crime scene.

And the first thing that hits me is, holy fucking shit. This is brutal even for me.

Now, I know it might seem overdramatic to turn up to a crime scene and get queasy. Me, Arthur, queasy. But this is quite a striking scene.

The John Doe is dead, that much is for certain, and his brain, or what's left of it, has been removed and placed on the floor next to his head. His hands have also been removed, as has his penis. And all four items are collected up quite nicely near his head. The head, which has been surgically cut open, has been placed back together haphazardly, and if you look carefully enough, you can see daylight through it.

I do that standard shocked person response and raise my hand to my mouth and gasp. I once returned to my car to find a dead person, guts and all, splayed all over the bonnet, but this is something else.

'You okay, Dad?' asks Olivia. And I nod. I feign gagging and walk away from the crime scene. I am no crime scene operative, so I will let these women and men do their work. I am also no brain surgeon—clearly—and I'm not saying that the new me is, but they have a certain aptitude for removing body parts, certainly with a precision that I don't possess. I stand at the back of the scene and wait for my daughter to join me: she does.

'See what I mean?' she asks. 'We can't see a world where a woman is doing this. Not on her own, at least.' I look around the small play park and think of how tainted the swing set will be now. A man will forever have died in this park. Is this the kind of knock-on effect my killing has on people's lives, even in the most remote of ways? And, Arthur, you're in your head again. You are here for your daughter. Focus, Arthur, focus.

'Do you have anything?' I ask.

'The victim was Paul Huntson. A convicted child molester. He was supposed to be staying well away from residential areas like this.'

'Do you think that's why the killer brought him back here?'

'And chopped off his dick?'

I look at Olivia, and she shrugs.

'What? It's not the first time that the Hacker has removed or damaged the offending body parts. We think it might have started accidentally, but he's certainly got a feel for it now.'

The new me is starting to leave a signature. I wanted to leave nothing, and this news is unwelcome. I understand leaving a message, but this clown is painting the town red. Not to mention that, but the bodies are now being left to be found.

'Are you sure these new bodies are linked with the old ones?' I ask. 'After all, it appears that they went to some effort to conceal the original ones.'

'They?'

'What?'

'You said "they" again, Dad. Do you propose that there is more than one of them?' I look at the scene and think it's entirely possible that I would need help orchestrating that.

I shake my head. 'No, sorry, figure of speech again.'

'We did consider this, Dad. But serial killers tend to have a natural trajectory. They kill and bury animals in their backyards as kids. Maybe he started by doing something similar. Maybe now he feels like he's perfected his craft, and now he's just showing off.'

'Any evidence?'

'Nothing useful so far. Certain tool marks. We are chasing them all down, but most of these things can be bought in hundreds of different places.'

Olivia nestles into me slightly, and it nudges me into a nearby oak tree. The movement dislodges an acorn, and it falls, hitting me on the head. The bump is small, but I look up, and as it hits me, it hits me.

Ta-da. I am like Newton. Struck by something falling from a tree. Serendipity hit me along with that acorn; it is then that my brain considers whether this is an inside job or not.

It would be feasible. They would have the know-how, the resources, the ability to stop people, the access to the criminal database, and the correct sense of moral justice. I pin that tab in my brain and turn to Olivia to speak.

'Now what?'

'Now we question any potential witnesses and head back to the police station. The crime scene techs will be here for a while. We'll only get in their way.'

*****

Questioning witnesses was exactly as boring as it sounded. Some might have legitimately seen something, but it occurred to me that most were just happy for something to break up the banality of their lives.

Happily, my daughter did all the talking, allowing me to fall back into my head.

And now we are pulling up at the station. It has been a long, exhausting, and slightly grizzly day, and I am thoroughly looking forward to going home.

Olivia slides her Twingo into the spot that my Alfa used to reside in, and she steps from her car. It is twenty to six, and by all accounts, time for Arthur to go home. But just as we exit the car, a familiar face appears from the building, and he soon finds himself in a discourse with Olivia.

'I'll get on them as soon as I start tomorrow morning,' he says. And then he places his hand on her shoulder and suddenly I know exactly why I recognise him. This is shoulder-grabbing hand man. The one I pictured throwing to the floor and stomping on his hand the day I met Olivia. I picture doing the same as I exit the vehicle and shuffle myself around it, so I am in earshot with them.

'Nigel,' says Olivia. 'This is my father, Arthur. Arthur, this is Nigel.'

Nigel! I think to myself. Fucking Nigel! I was not expecting that. I step toward him, thrust my hand out promptly like any normal person, and he repeats the gesture.

'Nigel here is our resident pathologist,' says Olivia as our hands continue to shake. The words slither sibilantly into my brain, and as I look him in the eye, I see a dark connection between us. And instantly, I know that there is something off about this man. The words register in my mind as our hands fall back to our side, and that's when it hits me: he's a pathologist.

'I guess you're pretty good with a bone saw, then?' I ask. *What, I've said weirder things.*

He nods. 'Pretty good. Hey, why don't you come down to the mortuary, and I'll show you.'

'You don't have to, Dad—' Olivia begins. But I cut her off.

'I'd love to!'

'Good, well,' says Nigel as he combs his slick black hair across his face. 'Come on down any day after ten.'

I nod. I look Nigel up and down. In close proximity, he is a formidable man. Six feet, maybe six-two. At least a hundred kilos and he clearly works out. He is a fraction shorter than me, but then I don't work out, and I'm in my sixties. He has a small scar next to his lip that exacerbates his smile lines, and at a push, he is handsome. His dark brown eyes remain locked on mine, and I can feel them trying to burrow into my skull. He grins once more, and it is as empty as mine, and then takes a step back towards his car. 'Good to meet you, Arthur,' he says as he moves away to his car.

'See you tomorrow, Nige,' says Olivia as she waves.

Nige! Fucking Nige? Here he is, Nigel, the pathologist, and I'm pretty sure he is the one running about dismembering bodies and here is my daughter, the police officer, calling him 'Nige'. So, one thing is for sure: we don't see people's darkness. Unless she does. Has she sensed it in me already?

I watch Nigel drive out of the car park, and alarm bells are ringing in my head. My daughter is too close to this. If Nigel does anything to harm a hair on my daughter's head, there will be no coming back for Nigels anywhere. The remaining few will be deleted from society in a mad rage fuelled by vitriol.

Anyway, it would seem the real Hampshire Hacker has been hiding in plain sight by working in forensics for the police—where have I heard that before?—and he is too close to all of this, and certainly too close to my fucking daughter. I look down and realise that both of my hands are clenched shut. Deep breaths, Arthur. In through the nose, out through the mouth.

TEN.

It's safe to say I couldn't sleep last night. I haven't been able to sleep any night this week. And no, the irony isn't lost on me. I couldn't sleep because my daughter is closer than she knows to the Hampshire Hacker, which is ironic, yes. Because she is close to both. Worlds have collided. This is like Kirk meeting Picard in Generations. The classic faces the newcomer.

And I wonder if he knows, too. Does Nigel know I am me?

Regardless, my priority right now is keeping my daughter safe—and it should have been all along. My mistake was thinking that my friends and family would be better off without me, all the while a wolf has been stalking my den. I thought I needed to leave to keep them all safe, but a new threat is on the horizon, and to make matters worse, it is now Saturday, and I have a date with my parents . . . and Olivia wants to come, too. It would seem she has a 'relationship' with her grandparents. Which annoys me more than it should. I think it is because I never really had one with them. Still, I shouldn't let an emotion as petty as jealousy get in my way.

I rise from the sofa, shelve my thoughts and look at the clock I have erected on the south wall of the house. It is just after ten a.m., and my daughter is meeting me here in minutes.

What a day today is going to be . . .

***

'Hello, mother,' I say as I walk through the front door. I place my hands on her tiny frame and hug her as dearly as I can.

'You could have got here earlier,' is literally the first thing she says to me.

'It's good to see you, too,' I reply. I look at my watch and consider it is half past one—the traffic was pretty bad.

'And what did you do to your hair?' she asks.

'Oh, I've missed you, too,' I say as I squeeze her as hard as I can. I look beyond her and into the spotless mirror in the hallway, and I look at my blond hair—what's left of it—and I consider that it could use a trim. I turn from the mirror and spot my father limping his way down the hallway. He is grey, he has shrunk, he is grumpy. I look at him, and I consider that he has completed the transformation into Droopy. And as per usual, I can't tell if he is happy to see me. It's been nearly twenty-six years; you'd like to think happiness prevails . . .

. . . But instead of saying anything, he looks at me and smiles. And he joins me and my mother in the world's most awkward hug.

We embrace, and then, when I free myself from what feels like hugging a box of jellyfish, I turn to the door and watch my daughter dance through it after parking the car—the drive is full because Judy is already here. I go to introduce her, and then I remember it is us that have only just met.

My father greets his granddaughter and then does his usual bit of shuffling off into the study, ready to get angry at inanimate objects whose only crime was doing what they were designed to do. I lead Olivia further into the house, and we catch our breaths in the kitchen. It's safe to say I would rather be doling out balls of yarn to a pride of lions than be here, but my parents are old . . . and I have been missing. My mum joins us in the kitchen, and she hugs me once more. Then she cracks open the fridge and pours me a gluten-free beer. I have heard that gluten-free products have come a long way in the last three decades, and with no Jenny to palm it off on, I accept it with a crooked smile.

'Oh, I didn't know you were gluten-free, Dad,' I do my best to shake my head and shake away any gluten-free notions, but I fail. And I see it register in my daughter's head that she must cater for me sans gluten.

Having never been blessed with tremendous social grace, I take a sip from my beer (which isn't all that bad) and ask my mum *who else is in attendance.*

'Everyone is here, Arthur. They are out on the deck with the heaters on.'

The deck!

The flipping deck.

My parents love their deck, and they make as much use of it as possible. It doesn't matter that it's England in March and the temperature is barely in the double figures . . . the whole family must sit on the deck.

'Define everyone?'

'Oh, Arthur, just take your daughter and go outside, will you?' My mother continues to shuffle around the kitchen, and seriously, how much longer can the two of them have?

I take Olivia by the hand (that's what dads do, right?), and I lead her away from the kitchen. We walk through the spotless hallway, into the lounge, passed the sofas, and finally out onto the deck. The assembled crowd rises as we arrive, and as Olivia doles out hugs to those in attendance, I stop and consider how weird it is that my daughter, whom I've just met, probably has a better relationship with my family than I do, and vice versa. I halt in the mouth of the French windows, take a deep breath, and look around. It is nice to be distracted from the Hampshire Hacker!

'Arthur,' comes a gruff but familiar voice.

'Aga,' I say as I move across the deck toward her large frame. Aga, or more correctly, Auntie Aga, is my Uncle Phil's second wife following his divorce. Unfortunately, for the children (who are not in attendance), she is not their birth mother . . . sorry gene pool. Aga is a larger-than-life character, and I love her dearly . . . or I would were she not somehow associated with this family.

'Arthur, you were dead?'

'It sure felt like it,' I say. We embrace, and I'm sure this is what being hugged by a brown bear feels like. We stop, and I check my limbs, which are all still attached. She reaches into her pocket and produces a pack of cigarettes, which she sneakily palms off on me. Ah, good. I know these to be a cheap Polish brand—extra nicotine, extra tar, extra cancer, extra death! She sits back down, and her husband, Phil, pipes up.

'Hi, Arthur,' he says.

'Hi, Phil,' I reply as we shake hands. Phil is a myrmidon. I know I am supposed to be feigning a limited capacity, but Phil has been struggling with limited capacity his whole life. I have no idea what Aga sees in him, but it happens—ask Melissa and Ophelia . . .

I relinquish Phil's hand just in time to see Judy approaching me. She pats me on the back and opens her mouth simultaneously.

'Arthur, you remember Charlene and Elizabeth?' A pair of thirty-something-year-olds appear as if by magic from behind Judy's back, and I take a step backwards. The twins! The creepy-fucking-twins . . . and I swear that everything they do is in unison! I get confused as I re-introduce myself to the twins, and before I know it, we are all sitting down on the deck in relative comfort. Of all the children (not children anymore) that could have been in attendance it had to be Judy's twins.

Judy was married, but she caught her husband, Tim, knee-deep in people he shouldn't have been—they got divorced. Judy, it would seem, has never been that interested in going again, and to be fair, I can see why not. It isn't easy when someone you thought you loved betrays your trust.

My wife, Melissa, was never dead . . . until she died . . . in a shoot-out with mercenaries in the New Forest (I know, I was there) anyway, I thought that Melissa was simply a very understanding lawyer who helped me pick up where the justice system left off. But in truth, she was a gun for hire herself. And as much as I did love her, I have had some rotten luck when it comes to the ladies.

My mother appears with food on trays, and my father follows her out shortly after. They set the food down, they sit, and we all stare at the food longingly. A stunted silence falls over the chilly deck, and an unexpected voice springs up from the cold.

'I just want to say how thankful I am to have my father back, especially at such a taxing time,' says Olivia. Those in attendance raise their glasses, and we all toast me.

Cheers, Arthur!

The evening is winding down. Most of us are drunk, except for Judy. I speak, and a slur spills from my mouth. My eye catches Judy's, and we are locked in a moment. It's like she is telling me she is watching me.

I guess it's fair; I am the resident serial murderer who has been in hiding for nearly three decades. I decided what was best for everyone (me), and then I decided what was best for me (me), and now I'm back in the lives of the people whose lives I ruined. And my girlfriend is dead. My wife is dead.

Jenny is dead . . . it's fair, I'd be watching me, too. I shoot Judy what I think is a wink, and I stand from my chair, pat my daughter on the shoulder and then meander down the deck's steps and into the concrete jungle that makes up the rest of the garden. Here I find Aga. Smoking.

'Hi, Aga,' I say.

'Arthur,' says Aga, who turns and beams at me. She grabs me as I arrive and suddenly, I am trapped in a hug—what's with people and hugs? I hold Aga as she holds me, and I consider how much older we all are. The last time I was here was nearly thirty years ago. So much has changed, and yet, for me, it has remained the same. My life has been on pause while everyone else moved on. I think about Ophelia as I consider 'moving on', and I wonder if she ever did.

'Where you been, Arthur?'

'Upstairs, with the others.'

'No, not tonight. For last thirty years, where you been?'

I have been doing my best to avoid this question, like a Conservative Party member when asked what they had to go without as a child. People know the official story, but I'm not keen on them asking.

'I don't remember,' I say.

'You don't remember, or you don't want to remember?'

Aga is being direct as always.

'Probably a bit of both.'

'Then why did you come back?'

I motion with my head towards the deck, and Aga says:

'Olivia.'

I nod.

'She is big girl, Arthur.'

'I know,' I say. 'But she needs me right now.'

Aga grunts, reaches into her coat pocket, produces a cigarette, lights it, takes a drag, and then hands it to me.

I take a drag myself, and the nicotine pervades my brain. It mixes with the alcohol, and everything speeds up. Suddenly, I wish I hadn't had so much to drink. I can feel my insides beginning to crawl back up, and maybe I shouldn't have come back. My daughter has now doubled her quota of serial killers in her life, and what if I'm the problem? Am I a safer bet? I ruined June's life—to be fair, it was already pretty ruined—Jenny died because of me, and I put everyone at risk. If I'm ever discovered, they will all be subjected to the most intense scrutiny. It doesn't matter how it looks; the general public will assume they must have known. And then there is Theo. Yes, he was a woman fondling degenerate, but I killed him in cold blood . . . there is no escaping that, is there?

'Arthur,' Aga's voice transcends my reverie, and I stare at the cigarette in my hand to see that it is all ash. She pats me on the back and then motions back towards the deck. I nod, extinguish what's left of my cigarette, and follow her inside.

Okay, now it's late. Aga and Phil have gone home, my father is back in the study torturing machines, and my mother is having her daily tidy. Judy is God knows where, and I am engaged in a tense game of Scrabble with one of the twins. I'll be honest: a night on the tiles means I can barely even see the tiles in front of me, and I'm not entirely sure which twin I'm playing with. Fortunately, she took up the job of scoring; unfortunately for me, from this drunken angle, I can't make out her name on the score sheet—not without my glasses.

And I cannot get out of my head. I need a distraction; the only ones I know start with a 'K' and end with 'ill'. But who, and how, and when? Working with the police means that a lot of my background is being scrutinised—that was always going to happen. But my past is fairly clean; thanks to Melissa, I've always done a good job of staying free. But she has long since passed away, and my carefully hidden bodies are being analysed in morgues across the county. I think the reality is that I am going to have to get this out of my system, and there really is only one eligible victim: me!

Well, not actual me, but the Hampshire Hacker part two. He is most definitely deserving of death; he is close by, and he is a danger. I will be killing a whole flock of birds with one stone. There is just one problem: he works for the police, and his disappearance will most definitely be noticed. Plus, if he is the Hampshire Hacker, if he disappears quietly in the night, the bodies will dry up, and that will leave the police with only one person to focus on . . . me.

My unnamed twin makes a move, and I see that it is the last of her tiles.

'Good game, Uncle Arthur,' she says. I go to speak, but suddenly, there are two twins in the room, and my night just got more complicated. If I take my eye off one, I might lose my focus, but on the other hand, I need to see what is written on this score sheet.

'Let me see that?' I say as I grab the small piece of paper. I look at the scores to see that I got thrashed, and I go to defend myself before I remember my objective here. 'Well done, Elizabeth,' I say, and I look up to see the pair of them staring at me. I look at my sister's offspring, and suddenly, all I can see is two versions of her—staring back at me, judging. Seeing two Judy's is weird. Both have our crooked nose, they both have blonde hair, and they both look just like younger Judy.

My Judy vision is only interrupted by the actual Judy entering the room, which is a pleasant surprise for once. She rallies the twins (and I swear everything they do is in unison), and before I know it, I am trapped in a double hug as they both say:

'Goodbye, Uncle Arthur.' I stand and match the twin's hug. As strange as they are, it is wonderful to be surrounded by my own family once more. I force away a tear from my eye, and I release myself from their embrace and turn to face Judy. The twins scamper out of the room—together—and I am left alone with Judy.

'Be careful, Arthur,' she says to me.

'I'm always careful, Jude.'

'Until you're not. Remember, I can't clean up after you. Not this time.' Olivia blunders her way into the room—she is visibly drunk—and she stumbles (quite literally) into our conversation.

'Who's clearing up?' she asks.

'Probably mother,' I say. Olivia giggles.

'Dad,' she says, 'I came to see if you want the guest room or the sofa?'

'I'll take the sofa, darling.'

'You sure? You are getting old.'

'Hey,' I say playfully, 'go to bed, young lady.' Olivia kisses me on the cheek and says *goodnight* to Judy as she departs the room. It's strange, we are in sync despite our differences. And I watch on in wonder as she leaves.

Judy watches on and says nothing. She grabs me and pulls me in close for a hug. And I feel like a boa constrictor is smothering me. But amid the crushing, she whispers in my ear.

'It's good to have you back, Arthur. Just don't fuck this one up!'

Then, she withdraws and departs the room like an apparition. And suddenly, I am alone.

ELEVEN.

The waking knowledge that Judy might have missed me hits me like a sledgehammer. Well, maybe that's the hangover. But still. My sister, missing me? My return seems to be rather triumphant. Never before did I think that a character such as myself might be missed. That somehow, people might want more. It's almost as though I am liked.

My ego falls as my headache rises, and I stumble from the sofa, open the patio doors, and meander out onto the deck. The sun is just about poking its head through the clouds, and I bask in it as I take a cigarette from my pocket.

I light, inhale, exhale and then consider my options. Do I persevere? It has been nearly thirty years since I claimed a life. But on the flip side, I have killed a lot of animals—a luxury I am no longer afforded in urban Southampton. Or do I get rid of the threat once and for all? Do I kill new me? It does serve the greater good, and it protects my daughter, which is important.

Having had my cigarette, I amble back into the house and greet my mother in the living room.

'Morning,' she says.

'Hello, mother,' I reply.

'Will you stay another night?'

I shake my head.

'Lots still to do, I'm afraid. But we'll be back down for father's birthday in June.' My mother nods, hugs me lightly, and then busies herself with finding something to clean. I wander from there into the kitchen, where I find my father pouring himself a cup of coffee—excellent, coffee was on the agenda.

'Morning, Dad,' I say. My father sets his mug down, looks up at me and smiles. Then he opens his mouth to speak:

'Arthur—' and that's it. He takes his coffee up in his hand and wanders out of the room. Excellent, stoicism fucking won again, as usual. That said, I don't know what I'm complaining about. I would rather stick my groin in a woodchipper than deal with undue emotion. Still, would it kill them to admit that they have missed me? Alone in the kitchen, I sit down to enjoy my piping hot beverage in peace. Or so I thought . . .

. . . Because forty seconds later, in bounces my larger-than-life daughter. Ah, the youth and their ability to shake off hangovers with a hot shower.

'Morning, Dad,' she beams. And it is still strange being called 'Dad.' Am I a dad?

The pressures of life are starting to get to me, and I grin a fractured grin back at my daughter.

Life is a dick! When I'm alone, I wish I wasn't, and when I'm with people, I wish I were alone. I can see why some serial killers go straight down the 'loner' route. I feel better for having my daughter back in my life—much better—but at the same time, it comes with a whole new box of problems. Problems I wouldn't have were I still living in a small wooden hut in the foothills of the Alps.

Still, I decided to return. So, I stand, hug my daughter and convince her that we must leave—soon. She agrees since her life is mainly work and even offers to drive the return leg. I wouldn't normally accept, but my head feels like it is entertaining a rave—and I fucking hate raves!

We sashay through the pleasantries of leaving, and then, before I know it, we are standing on the doorstep saying our goodbyes. My mother and father hug me simultaneously, something which feels like getting to second base with a herd of wildebeest, and then they say goodbye to my daughter. Judy's car takes up the driveway, so we take the short walk down the hill and go in search of my car—Judy accompanies us. Being young, Olivia walks on ahead, leaving Judy and me alone as we walk and talk.

'Do you know what you're doing?'

'Does anyone, Jude.'

'Don't be coy, Arthur. You're playing a dangerous game.'

I nod, turn to face Judy, and notice that her face has pulled itself into some weird expression—it might even be concern.

'Don't do that with your face, Jude!' She scowls, but it isn't long before her mouth opens again.

'I'm serious. I need to know you have your shit together. I can't protect you like last time.'

'Don't worry,' I say.'

'That's exactly what worries me.'

I smile my most confident fake smile at Judy, and we continue down the road towards the car.

***

Being alone was a choice. A choice, okay. But it didn't come lightly. I thought that everyone was better off without me in their life. I mean, everyone needs that one weird friend with their kinks and eccentricities, but not everyone needs a sociopathic killer in their life. But it would seem (stoicism aside) that I have been missed, even by Judy . . . and Judy knows what I am.

Regardless, it's a choice I made and one I have to stick with. But reintegrating myself with people is proving to be a challenge. I got used to only serving the needs of Arthur, not needing permission, and not saying very much. And as much as I enjoy being back, I do still carry a flame for my old life.

Still, there is no sense dwelling. Today is a new day; today is Monday. I managed to convince my daughter that I needed to get to grips with the inner workings of the police station while she would be out interviewing witnesses . . . which is great because it affords me the time to get acquainted with Nigel . . .

I shit, shower, and shave, and then I move towards the door. I see myself in the mirror by the door and stop. I see that a smile has nearly painted itself all over my face, and I remember why: this week's weather forecast looks to be cloudy with a chance of murder. . . .

I arrive at the police station and park up in my space outside—not a sentence I ever thought I would say. I even have my little ID card now. It would seem my background check came back negative.

Just the one arrest . . . for murder. But I was exonerated, and it's partly because of that I'm here. The weird twists of fate, huh? At one point, I was hours away from going to jail for Theo's murder (and certainly many more now) and yet here I am helping the police as a concerned citizen who was one of the last people to see Theo alive. The fact that I was exactly the last person to see him alive notwithstanding.

I walk into the building and force a fake smile onto my face. Despite being a relatively new building in the 2000s, it hasn't aged well. There are phones with cables on them, and most of the décor is off-brown. I would be depressed, but I have other things on my mind . . . and it would seem they have me in mind, too. I am in the building for less than ten minutes when Nigel knocks on the wall of my cubby hole, and he suggests *I join him down in the mortuary.*

I couldn't be more in agreement and before I know it, I am on my feet and hot on the heels of my new friend Nigel.

The forensic morgue is grey, slabby and cold. Nigel leads me into his lair, and before he says anything, he opens a drawer.

HolyfuckingshitNigel!

Seeing a frozen corpse was not the first thing on my agenda for today, and despite my many grizzly adventures, it takes all the restraint I have not to bring up my breakfast!

The body slides out of the drawer like a zip on a jacket, and before I know it, I am face to face—ish—with the body of a young female. Her torso already features the 'Y' incisions that I am familiar with—familiar from the fucking TV—and from what I can tell, she has been bludgeoned to death.

'Beaten to death with the television remote!'

As if sensing what I was thinking, Nigel chimes in.

'Why?' I ask him, in the hope that he would answer the latter question as well as why he fucking opened a drawer and showed me a fucking corpse!

'Deadbeat boyfriend, he's out on bail at the moment. The guy has money; I wouldn't be surprised if he hires a fancy lawyer and pleads the charges down.'

'To what?' I ask, almost in disbelief.

'Self-defence. Involuntary manslaughter.'

'Involuntary?' I mumble to myself. 'How old was she?'

Nigel sits down in a wheeled chair; once there, he wheels across to his desk and grabs a file from the locked drawers next to it. Then he wheels back across the room, the chair clunks over the tiled floor, and he arrives opposite me on the other side of the body.

'27,' he says cooly.

I don't have time for it to register in my brain before a phone rings in the other room.

'I have to get that,' says Nigel. He sets the file down next to the corpse, raises himself from his chair, and walks casually into the next room.

Once he is out of my sight, the folder calls out to me. The victim is not much older than my daughter, and the perpetrator is out there living his best life while this poor girl lies dead on a table. I don't consider this fact for long before the siren song of the manilla folder calls out to me. I reach (carefully) over the body, grab the folder and then open it up to read.

By the time Nigel reappears, the folder is back in its original space, the contents firmly burned into my mind, and suddenly, I have grand plans for the rest of this week . . .

The thought of murder is exciting!

I know. I know; I've been toying with the idea of not killing people. But this just fell into my lap. Removing women-killing dickheads from the world is exactly the sort of thing I was made for.

The folder—thanks, Nigel—gave me everything I needed to know about my perp. It has also given me a reprieve from my head and thoughts of dispatching Nigel—sorry, Nigel.

The good news is that my eligible victim, Matt Goodwin, lives in Southampton. The bad news is that he shares a flat with a friend. The fact that a lowlife like Matt has friends aside, the roommate situation makes it harder for me to get Matt alone.

But I am nothing if not resourceful, so I work with what I have got. And what I have is a mighty lizard brain and the experience that comes with having done this dozens and dozens of times . . .

. . . I've followed Matt to work. Matt works in a god-awful pub in the arse-end of Southampton. In a place called Lordshill, which is an ironic name. The pub fits right in with the general aesthetic—in that it looks like shit—and everything is depressing . . . everything except my thoughts. You see, for once, everything is red and rosy in the world of Arthur. It has been nearly twenty-six years since I did this, and I couldn't be more excited!

I wait outside 'The Bull' pub until closing time. Waiting is boring, but before long, I see my man walking out of the front door before locking it. He performs very cursory checks of the building before leaving.

Oh, that's right, I am lying in the back of Matt's car. What, too cliché?

Matt has a 1999 Ford Mondeo; breaking into it was one of the easiest things on earth. Partly because the car doesn't have central locking, and poor Matt failed to lock all the doors. But my ingenuity saw me try the doors first, and now here I am, just waiting for Matt.

Matt walks over to the car. He lights a cigarette as he walks, and I duck down behind the cover of the door—lest he sees me. Matt arrives, and the door opens.

The smell of tobacco permeates the car, and I am forced to cover my mouth lest I cough. Tobacco has been having that effect on me lately, and maybe I should see a doctor.

I shelve thoughts of my health and advancing age, and I bring myself back to the fore. Matt slides in like he owns the place—maybe he does—and places his head on the headrest. I go to make my move, but suddenly, something doesn't add up! Nigel told me this guy had a fancy lawyer, and none of this makes sense financially.

I don't have time to dwell on my revelation before Matt shifts in his seat and adjusts the rear-view mirror. I can only assume that something caught his eye, and he adjusted the mirror so that it is looking directly at me. I am hidden in the semi-darkness of the backseat, but it is still pretty obvious when you have a full-grown man lying across the rear bench. Matt spots me immediately, and I am forced into action; I don't give him time to cause a ruckus, and I sit up, bolt forward, grab his neck from behind and give it a firm twist. Matt's neck snaps with a satisfying *crunch,* and suddenly, the car is silent. A distant flash catches my eye, but upon looking out, I see nothing—perhaps a storm is due?

I slink out of the car, leaving Matt's body as it is. The evening didn't quite go to plan, but bad Matt is dead, and I can only hope that the police chalk his murder up to just another death by the Hampshire Hacker. It is handy having someone masquerade as me. It fits the bill.

I walk at a steady pace back to my car, removing the hat as I do. For once, the temperature in England is actually to my advantage and I am not too hot when I stuff the garment in my pocket. I whistle as I walk, and I exhale; I look up at the sky and grin.

God, it feels good to be back!

TWELVE.

Midway back to my car, my phone rings. A lot is going on right now, so I dig deep into my pocket, retrieve my phone and place it to my ear.

'Hello,' I say.

'Arthur,' says my good friend Rich Richard. 'What are you doing tomorrow?'

I pause.

I should have an excuse, but I have just killed a man from behind while he sat in his car, and I don't have the time to be creative right now.

'Nothing, why?'

'Come and play golf with me!'

I pause again.

I've got nothing.

'Golf? Tomorrow?'

'Excellent, I'll text you the deets, and I'll see you there.'

I grimace. And just as I'm about to remove the phone from my ear, Richard pipes up again.

'Oh, and Arthur, make sure you dress appropriately, yeah?'

Rich Richard hangs up, and I turn a corner and hurry back to my parked car. This isn't the first time I have made this mistake, and I really should have learned by now.

It looks like I'm playing golf tomorrow.

I make it to the car and turn back. All is quiet, and no one followed me. I unlock the door (with the key), get in, and sigh.

Boy, what a day tomorrow is going to be . . .

***

Golf is a ridiculous sport!

Well, maybe it isn't. But something about having to dress ready to be overthrown by the French general public doesn't add up, and there should definitely be cake!

I arrive at the golf course and pull into the car park; I haven't felt this overdressed since I tackled Jarrod, the cat vivisector, in his attic, dressed in all-black overalls. The car park surface is made up of just shingle, and the Alfa's powerful wheels spin over it like a propellor, sending stones flying in various directions.

I park up and enter the building. Rich Richard is waiting for me, sporting a boisterous grin, and I'm not sure either of us can look more ridiculous. It is classed as a 'sport', so I thought we would be dressed for a sporting occasion and not a Bah Mitzvah.

'Arthur, you made it!'

Yes, Richard, I made it. I wouldn't be standing here if, in fact, I hadn't made it!

'Anytime,' I say.

Richard picks up his golf bag and points to the one I assume is mine (I don't own golf clubs), and we wander toward our first tee. We talk as we walk, and Richard says,

'Been up to much?'

I consider my evening, and as much as I would love to unburden myself, I don't see Richard still wanting to play golf with me after having told him about how I snapped someone's neck last night . . . but it would get me out of golf.

I make inoffensive small talk as we bluster through the first few rounds. One thing is for sure: golf is a very 'swingy' sport, and I definitely should have warmed up for this. We make it as far as hole four before Richard pipes up again. It would seem that he is far better at this 'sport' than I am (he is rich; it comes with the territory).

'So how is . . . you know?'

I shake my head.

'How is what, Richard?'

'God, yes, that's right. Fatherhood.'

'It's good, Richard, but not without its challenges.' I pause and ponder. I don't add the part about trying to track down the killer who is posing as me so that I can, well, kill him to protect my daughter.

'We tried to. You know . . .' says Richard.

This time, I do kind of know. And short of a better plan, I place my hand on his shoulder and sort of clamp at it.

'What happened?' I ask ruefully.

'Well, we tried, Cathy and I, but it just wasn't meant to be.'

'What about adoption?'

'God, no,' says Richard. 'I wanted to continue the bloodline, Arthur.'

I nod. I remember that money is most of Richard's flaws and that, deep down, he is a very good guy. But who am I to judge? I killed a man after work—afterwards, for God's sake. The humane thing would have been to have killed him before! Perhaps I am a monster.

We plough through a few more rounds before I get my ball lost in the woods. I trudge over and look for it, but it is like finding a small white ball in, well, a thick brush. Shortly after, I give up. It is an apt metaphor, though. I am hiding. People are looking for me. I have killed based on limited information. My daughter is also chasing me, and to make matters worse, I am helping her. Life was certainly much simpler when I hid out in the French Alps, but boy was it fucking cold.

Richard allows me to use a new ball, and our golfing adventure continues until we reach the nineteenth hole.

'Drink?' says Richard.

And I should have known. Of course, the nineteenth hole would be some sort of golf-based joke. But we are now, at least, in a bar and I could very much use a drink.

THIRTEEN.

Golf was hard work.

And now, I am back at work!

This is not something I thought I would readily say. But work does allow me to spend some time with my daughter. It also offers me potential kills—like Matt—and insight into the killings of the Hampshire Hacker, aka me and probably Nigel. It does feel weird to be working alongside the potential new me, and as much as my gut tells me that it is him, I need to find some proof.

But first coffee!

The coffee here is dreadful. But it is at least free. I take a sip of my free coffee, and then I meander back to my small cubby hole and sit down at the table that has been deemed a 'desk'. There is a folder sitting on the surface, and I presume someone has something interesting for me . . .

. . . Okay! This might be problematic. Someone does, indeed, have something interesting for me. You see, I opened the folder and nearly spat out my coffee. The contents of the folder are me! Just me. Snapping a man's neck. From behind. In an old Ford Mondeo!

Yup. After all these years, I have been caught on camera.

And I knew it didn't add up, but what was I supposed to do? Matt saw me. There is no easy explanation for being in the back of a man's car . . . so I killed him. This is RIP Theo all over again. Except Theo truly was a cunt, so I hope he is resting in pain. That aside, I may have killed an innocent person, and perhaps all is not well in my brain! I have been so blinded by meeting (and protecting) my daughter that I didn't stop to do any research.

Plus, one thing is painfully obvious! Nigel set me up . . .

Nigel! Fucking Nigel. I have officially been framed by a Nigel, and is this what my life has come to?

Nigel.

I can't even think of any good Nigels. There was one in the British political system for a while. And we all know how that turned out . . .

On the upside, the folder on the desk would imply that this is to be kept a secret . . . for now. The bad news is that Nigel is probably not only the Hampshire Hacker (2.0), but he now has me on the hook. If he is any good (which I assume he is), then he has copies of this ready to be released should anything happen to him. And as much as I can accept my fate (I am a murderer), I have only recently got to know my daughter, and I am very much interested in spending more time with her. Something which won't be all that possible from jail. I mean, it won't be quality time, will it?

Oft, this is a hassle—one I could do without. But one thing is for sure: I have to go and see Nigel.

'What do you want?' is the first thing I ask Nigel upon storming into the morgue.

Nigel has company, but she takes one look at my face and says: 'I'll leave you to it!' before swiftly departing. I didn't get a good look at her because I was angry. Granted, this could be handled differently, but I am not meek. I am a killer of men, and I do not like being fucked with!

'You got my picture then?' he simpers.

'What do you want?' I repeat.

'Oh, come on, Arthur, where is your sense of adventure?'

'What do you want?'

'You! I want you.'

Nigel's words catch me off guard, and I am forced to readjust.

'You what?'

'Arthur, do you think I don't know exactly who you are? You might have fooled everyone else with the whole "I didn't kill Theo Richards" thing. But I know it's you.'

I look around the morgue in silence.

'Oh, don't worry, we are quite alone,' says Nigel. 'Unless you count the dead. Even Matt is in here. I gotta say, I admire your handiwork. How many people have you killed now?'

The words sneak into my brain and compliments aside; I am not enthused.

'Well, I don't think much of yours.'

'Arthur, this game requires a little showmanship, don't you think?'

'No!' I reply. 'I don't do this for fun.'

'Neither do I, Arthur. But this whole brooding loner I kill for good but don't tell anyone about it is boring. We should be celebrated for what we do. How many degenerates have we taken off the street, you and I?'

'Not enough,' I menace.

'Arthur, you're a smart man. You know what will happen to that photo if anything happens to me. What will dear Olivia think when she finds out that Dad is the Hampshire Hacker? What will it do to her career, her life?'

I throw my head upwards and glare at the tiles in the roof. Nigel has me by the bollocks, and he knows it. The roof distracts me from the many medical implements which could be used to remove Nigel's head from his shoulders, and I breathe in and out. In through the nose, Arthur. In through the nose.

'What do you want?' I say once more with contrition.

'There he is—the big bad Hacker. What I want, Arthur, is a little fun. You and me. The Hampshire Hackers as one.

Think of all the good we can do. Think of all the fun we can have.'

'I—'

'Think about it, Arthur. Think about it for your daughter's sake. I mean, you were all too happy about snapping Matt's neck. I say we take your aptitude for killing and my showmanship on the road. We have everything we need right here,' he says as he taps on a stack of brown folders.

'Okay, fine,' I say. Nigel has me in a corner. And the closer he is to me, the safer I am. I need time to work out what he has in store for me and where he keeps the evidence, and then I can get rid of him. The threat has presented itself to me; now, I need to figure out how to get rid of it. It's just a puzzle, Arthur. You like puzzles. A puzzle with a bit of murder thrown in . . . it could be worse!

FOURTEEN.

I gave Nigel my phone number (grudgingly) and then swiftly departed the morgue. I have to admit, his attitude towards killing does impress me, but I am not certain about him, and I certainly don't appreciate being blackmailed. Nigel will find out the hard way that he fucked with the wrong person.

But that is for another day.

Today it is dinner with Abdul, Maureen, and my lovable daughter.

The problem with living a life that is a lie is that you are never sure how people feel about you. For example, Abdul, Maureen, Rich Richard, Cathy, Olivia, and my parents/family all love me, but they don't know me—not really. Would they all feel the same if they knew the truth about me? It doesn't quite keep me up at night, but I'm not certain about any of my relationships. Rachel Dawes couldn't live with Bruce Wayne being Batman. And she did love him. How will everyone deal with the real me?

'Bro-man Empire,' says Abdul, 'you've been very quiet tonight.' I raise my wine glass to my mouth and imbibe a large amount. The truth is I am distracted; Nigel—fucking Nigel—knows more about the real me than my best friend. I want to tell him. I do. But there is no conceivable way he still loves me the way he does once he knows I am the Hampshire Hacker—none of them will.

'I'm okay,' I reply. 'Just tired. This one has been keeping me busy at work.' I set my glass down on the table and then ruffle Olivia's hair as though she were twelve. Olivia looks across at me and smiles.

'Well, I'm all for it,' says Maureen. 'It's about time you got yourself a hobby.'

'Hey,' I say, defending myself. 'It's more than a hobby. Plus, I play squash and go to the gym . . . allegedly,' I add, remembering that I'm not supposed to remember.

'Dude,' says Abdul, looking at my midriff, 'when was the last time you played squash?' We all share in a laugh, and Maureen raises herself from her chair and sets about collecting the empty dinner plates.

'So, how is the case going?' asks Abdul. Maureen whacks him on the arm on her way out of the room, but he persists anyway.

'Not great,' says Olivia. 'I can't go into the specifics, but we aren't getting very far. I don't suppose you have any leads, do you, Uncle Abdul?'

Abdul shakes his head and laughs at the same time. I fall back into my head so hard that I almost miss the 'Uncle' moniker altogether. It's annoying; I know exactly who the Hampshire Hacker is. But I am not at liberty to tell anyone. There are so many secrets dotting about my brain, and it is hard not letting any of them slip.

Surprise! It's me. I'm one of the Hampshire Hackers. Hahaha. Can we all still be friends, please?

I concede that I'm being too hard on myself and that I'm doing the best I can with what I have, and I slip out of my reverie and back into the room.

'We'll get there,' I say as I face Olivia again. 'I believe in Team Norman!' *Team Norman? What the fuck did I just say?*

'I hope so,' says Olivia. 'This guy has been at large for too long!'

'Or girl,' adds Abdul helpfully. Maureen reappears from the kitchen, sporting a tray full of eclairs, and the evening moves on.

***

I wake the next morning to full-body stiffness, and then I remember that I agreed to swing metal sticks about with Rich Richard—hence the stiffness. There has to be a better use for metal sticks . . .

Rich Richard has aged horribly and well simultaneously. Most of his dark hair is gone, and the paunch increases every month. But a lifetime of being rich, spa days, and just generally being pampered has increased his longevity. He abuses the fuck out of his body and then submits it to serious intensive care.

I have no such luxury. It is a Saturday, and it is almost April. Spring is springing, and there should be a general feeling of optimism in the air, but there is not.

Today is very far from optimistic. This is because I had a text from my new friend Nigel—last name as yet unknown—telling me to meet him at West Quay shopping centre and to 'Bring my knives'!

One, how does he know I have knives? Luckily for him, I have already been out and bought a new set.

Two, West Quay Shopping Centre on a Saturday is a nightmare at the best of times. Bringing knives is less than ideal.

Nigel is out of his fucking mind.

But persevere, we must. Nigel not only knows the truth about me, but he could (massively) spoil things between me and Olivia. Nigel will get his comeuppance—in good time. For now, I must go along with the game . . .

I throw my knives in the back of the Alfa and set off into town. Fortunately, my new domicile is a mere ten minutes from West Quay, so I take a leisurely drive into town and fall into my head as I do.

On one hand, this is disastrous. I am being cajoled into killing by the Hampshire Hacker Junior. I kill because I have to.

But on the other hand, we do seem to share the same ethos . . . and it might be nice to have a partner of sorts.

But I am being blackmailed. And there is a lot on the line here. I am the definition of conflicted. But I do need to exorcise my dark tendencies. I park the Alfa in the multi-storey car park and wander inside. I leave the knives in the car (for now), and I check my phone to see what the update is from my pal Nigel. He tells me to meet him at Slim's Chicken in the food court, and I put my phone away and prepare to enter Hell.

West Quay is a gauntlet on a Tuesday lunchtime. On Saturday, it may as well be Valhalla (only more commercial). And the hallways cannot accommodate 800 people walking side-by-side and the only option is to try and swallow your arms. It is excessively 'shovey', and I have a very low tolerance for being shoved. I am not a fan of the general public at the best of times. It's safe to say that I would rather run naked through barbed wire than deal with an enclosed shopping precinct at the weekend. But we do what we must for those we love (Olivia), and I shelve my thoughts and slide into my happy place as I traverse the walkway along and up to the food court.

I slalom through the throngs of people, and I meet Nigel at the food court. He is eating from Slim's Chicken and hasn't thought to order me anything!

I slide into the super sticky seat situated near him and sit myself down so that I am opposite. He masticates on a grizzly piece of chicken, and for a moment, I get to see all of his teeth in their meat-riddled glory. He has one gold tooth, and I swear it flashes at me. The rest of his face is just creepy. He's a decent-looking bloke, but something about his features are off. It's like looking at the word 'Pepsi' in Coca-Cola's writing. And I'm not happy with it. His hair is black or very dark brown and neatly pasted to his head with wax, or dare I say hair 'gel'. He has one ear pierced with a small skull earring, and nothing else about him is remarkable.

'What are we doing here?' I ask as he continues to chew.

'Lunch, Arthur. We're getting lunch!'

'But why here?'

'Oh,' says Nigel cheerfully as he turns and looks over his left shoulder, 'well, you see that man over there? He's kidnapped, tortured and abused, then killed seven students. Three men, four women. He follows them home after nights out, kills them, and then somehow tosses their bodies in one of the local parks.'

'And you know this how?' I ask incredulously.

'I just know, Arthur. Just as sure as you knew who I was when you met me.'

'Bullshit,' I say, refusing to believe that it's possible to pick up on an innate darkness.

'I know it, Arthur. Just as you know it.'

'What's his name?' I ask.

'Alan,' replies Nigel.

'Alan?' I repeat. 'Fucking Alan?'

Nigel nods.

I stare beyond Nigel and into the eyes of Alan as he works away behind the counter of a small Harry Ramsden's. His eyes meet mine for a second, and I do know. I see directly into his soul, and it calls out to me.

And then it dawns on me. Do others see me the same way? Do people like Nigel stare into my eyes and see a cold-hearted killer? Do they think we are the same? Because I am nothing alike, am I?

'You see?' Nigel's voice crashes through my brain like Miley Cyrus on a wrecking ball, and I am jolted back to the fore. To say I've been questioning myself a lot lately would be an understatement.

I nod, and I do see. I do see, Nigel. I see that you are a problem, too. You and Alan share the same look, the same inner darkness, and I need you gone: both of you.

'We can't kill him here,' I whisper across the table.

'Obviously, Arthur. I'm just showing you who he is. But I know you need this, so how and when we will kill him is up to you!' I swallow, and it dawns on me that this is real. I need Nigel to disappear. But I don't know what he has on me or where. As much as Nigel needs to vanish, what he has on me can't just show up. I do the best with what I have—I do. And my daughter and my friends need me. I tried leaving them once, but they weren't better off without me. I need to be there for them, and Nigel poses a threat to them and me. So, I will kill Alan, and in the meantime, I will find out where Nigel keeps his dirt.

My throat finally clears enough to speak, and I squeak an *okay* in the direction of Nigel. He nods and then draws his cup, with a soggy paper straw, up to his lips and takes a sip.

And seriously, when can we invent a drinking utensil that lasts more than one minute but less than an eternity?

Nigel swallows his drink, stands, pushes away from the table and extends his hand out to me. Without thinking, I grab it, and he almost hauls me to my feet. Then, we shake hands. Nigel's grip is strong, and suddenly, I'm feeling like the older gentleman I am. Nigel finally lets my hand fall from his vice-like grip, and then he turns and moves away from the table, but not before stopping, turning back and saying: 'Come on, Arthur, let's go shopping!'

Now, if someone had told me I would be spending my time browsing lingerie, with Nigel from fucking work, in West Quay shopping centre, I would have thought they were having an aneurysm. Or at least I'd be thinking about causing one—somehow. That would be a handy skill to possess as a serial killer trying to stay free of the law.

Which is not what Nigel is doing! HE is putting bodies on display for all to see. HE has taken the Hampshire Hacker moniker and made it into a spectacle. I now have to kill someone at his behest, in tandem with him. But I am short on options here, and Alan does look like a menace.

Nigel stops us in front of a lacey 'teddy' and says, 'What do you think?'

'I think it's a bit small!'

'Ahh, good one, Arthur,' says Nigel as he punches at my arm. The hit to the arm smarts somewhat, and I do hope that lingerie shopping and arm punches aren't going to be a thing during our (hopefully) short friendship.

'No, for Grace!' he says.

'Grace?' I utter in disbelief.

'Yeah, my wife, Grace,' utters Nigel. I pause in thought and stare at the teddy in front of me. I hadn't stopped to consider that Nigel might have a wife. I had assumed— mainly from his looks—that he'd be a loner. How very judgmental of me.

The fact that Nigel has a spouse catches me out, and I am forced to say, 'It looks very tasteful!'

'Thanks, Arthur. It does, doesn't it?' says Nigel.

Nigel grabs the lacey garment from the rack, and before I know it, we're at the till. Nigel produces an Amex, a fucking Amex? And not long after that, we are on the move. Nigel walks me back to the multistorey car park, pulls me in for a hug, and then gets straight into his car, which was parked in a disabled bay (no badge) and Nigel needs to hurry up on his way to Hell. Nigel's car, with him, disappears into the halls of the car park, and suddenly I am alone.

The feeling of being alone hits me hard. I could see Abdul, Olivia, Rich Richard, or even my sister. But I can't tell any of them about what's happening. Okay, Judy knows the real me. But I'm supposed to be behaving. She won't understand how I got mixed up in this. No one will understand. The only person who probably truly comprehends is Nigel. And he's a fucking lunatic.

For the first time since returning, I miss Ophelia. I even miss Melissa. For all her flaws, she came through for me in the end, and her intentions were always semi-good. I miss not having someone I can talk to. And my god, I feel alone.

I walk soberly towards the car and consider my daughter. She and I share so much; can it be that we really share this, too? Can she ever really know me? As much as I'm enjoying my relationship with her, I know it is fake. What I'm not telling her is enough for her to run away very far, right?

I reach the car and get in. The whole day has been dark and sobering, culminating in underwear shopping with Nigel (a colleague). I don't know how I feel about being lumped in with the other maniacs, and I have no one to talk to about it— no one at all.

I start the engine and pull away.

Tomorrow can only get better, surely?

FIFTEEN.

Having spent the latter part of Saturday being morose, I wake up sporting a general feeling of self-loathing, and it takes me an age to drag my ageing frame from bed.

Once up, I take to my computer and grab my phone as it sets about starting up.

What's Nigel's last name?

Is the WhatsApp message I shoot my daughter. I pause and consider that it's a bit of a weird message, and so I add:

I want to add him on Facebook.

That's what colleagues do, right? Work together for a small amount of time and then shoot the other a 'friend request', which the other has to begrudgingly accept lest it make things awkward.

Olivia doesn't take long to reply to me, and I discover that Nigel's surname is Dawson.

Nigel.

Nigel-fucking-Dawson.

Then I set about typing his name into Facebook, and the first result is very clearly my Nigel, and he is sporting a gigantic magnifying glass which he is holding up to the camera. Ignoring the fact that Nigel is an even bigger twat than I'd given him credit for, his profile is very sparse. But there is one telling piece of information that says he is married to Grace Dawson. I click on her profile, and the first picture is her timeline; it is a memory she has shared from five years ago that is captioned:

'Our one-year anniversary at Tenby Close!', and then the post goes on to say that they have been there ever since. Grace's profile doesn't have the same privacy settings— clearly. I can even zoom into the photo of the pair of them smiling and holding keys, and I can see that the house number behind Nigel's head says number thirty-one.

31 Tenby Close.

The amount of information some people put on the Internet never ceases to amaze me.

Safe in the knowledge that I know where Nigel resides, I go back to his profile and click on the 'Add Friend' button. The last thing I want is to be Nigel's Facebook friend. Especially when it comes to be known that he is the Hampshire Hacker, but I can act suitably shocked, and we do what we must to cover our tracks. With the computer finally awake, I take to Google Maps and look up Nigel's address. To my delight, his house is a mere five minutes from mine, so I log off the computer, swivel about in my chair and stand. I march towards the door and grab my coat, and before I know it, I am in the car and on my way to Nigel's.

Nigel's house is nice. Just nice. It looks like a two-up and two-down and has a small front lawn and a garage. Well done, Nigel. Having pulled up across the street from the front door, I settle in and wait.

Waiting is terribly boring, and it wouldn't be a stretch to say I would rather do the bleep test in Nigel's road, naked, than sit here and wait for him and his wife to leave the house . . .

. . . But leave, they do. And I am finally alone and free to access Nigel's domicile.

I sneak across the street as best I can. It's difficult to not belong and even harder to act like you do. But I make it across the street unmolested, ignore the front door, and head straight for the back. I don't have to turn over many rocks until I find one that contains a key to unlock the back door and slide inside.

I close the patio doors and look around. To say that Nigel's house is gaudy would be an understatement. There is a wooden 'Live. Love. Laugh.' sign on the mantelpiece, and I already hate them both. Above the sign is a giant picture of Nigel and Grace. They are hugging, but it couldn't be more awkward if it tried. Other than that, there are two sofas, both of which are covered with throws and an open-plan kitchen behind them. The fridge appears to have a mind of its own and burbles away interminably. Having wasted time admiring their living room/kitchen, I depart and go in search of the study. It is not a big house, because who in the UK can afford a big house, and it doesn't take me long to locate Nigel's domain, which might sound sexist. But the study door does, literally, have a sign on it that denotes it as 'Nigel's Domain!' Fucking Nigel. Ignoring the douchey sign, I open the door and step inside.

And if I were expecting to see something grizzly with all of Nigel's best-laid plans out on show for all to see, I would be out of luck. Because Nigel's study looks like, well, a study. I sit down in Nigel's boring study, and I try the computer. It is password-protected, so I don't even try, and then, when everything seems lost, I see a sticky note that is attached to the desk. It says: Panda1999, and suddenly I am in.

The computer doesn't give much away, but I open Google Maps and check all his recent journeys. There is little there that is revolutionary, but there is an address that I don't recognise. I zoom in on the area to discover that it is a block of garages. And where else would a serial lunatic keep his supplies? I used to do the exact same—stuff that has probably since been long sold off on some reality TV show. I close the current tabs and then shut the computer down. Once off, I leave Nigel's Domain and descend the stairs. There is a key rack near the front door, and it doesn't take me long to analyse the keys. There is a small key on an estate agent's lanyard that also says number forty-one. I garner that it must be for Nigel's garage, and not wanting to outstay my welcome, I sneak out the rear door, replace the key in the fake rock, and return to the car. I am in it with the door closed before I can relax, and I throw my head back against the cool Italian leather.

It looks like I have a garage to check out.

***

Since it is a Sunday, and I assume Nigel hasn't taken his wife on a romantic trip to see his killing room (garage), I put the address into the car's in-built Sat Nav and set off to find Nigel's garage. The downside is that it is a Sunday, and others may be in attendance. Not good when I am going to have to break in. But it is always good to do one's research, so I set off in the direction of the garage regardless.

All this sleuthing is starting to feel a little like police work. This is weird, given that I am not only a police consultant, but I have literally solved their crime for them. I assume that one (some) of my bodies was discovered and that Nigel, being the pathologist, was the one who analysed it. I can only further assume that once the motive (loose motive) was established, he then took it upon himself to assume the mantle of Hampshire Hacker . . . and get creative with it. Perhaps his intentions were good; after all, he is dealing with filth that has eluded the law in some way. Regardless, he is a loose cannon, one that resorts to blackmail no less, so he must be dispatched. I will feel for Grace slightly, but on the flip side, I will be saving her from a serial lunatic.

I do wonder if people will think the same of me.

My reverie ends as I pull up in the vicinity of Nigel's garage and I leave the car over the road from the block and continue on foot. Being a classic only serves to make my car less than conspicuous, and I park it out of the way of the general public lest *focuspower999* pops out of the bushes to talk 'cars' with me. I am not in the mood to be noticed.

The block of garages is refreshingly empty, and I make straight for number forty-one. I am not accosted as I arrive, and I slip the crowbar I had grabbed from the car out of my sleeve and begin the task of prying the garage open. Fortunately, no prying eyes arrive as I perform my task and within a few minutes, I have the garage door ajar.

Call it professional courtesy, but I don't want the whole world to see Nigel's sins. There is also the small matter of me. I don't want people to see me breaking into a lunatic's garage—I could do without that scrutiny. Leaving a small gap at the bottom, I crouch down and crawl between the door and the frame. Once inside, I grab my phone from my pocket and shine it around in search of a light switch. Fortunately, it would seem that Nigel likes it to be well-lit when he kills people, and I find a light switch on the wall near the door. I flick it on, and the overhead halogens flicker into life. The light flickers, and I get glimpses of what is in the garage in between the darkness.

And what I see beggars belief.

I almost can't believe my eyes.

Nigel's garage contains perhaps the last thing I expected to see. Something so shocking that I don't know what to do with myself.

You see, Nigel's garage is almost bare, with a large tarpaulin covering an object in the middle of the floor. An object I am sure I recognise. I slip the cover off and then stand there in disbelief.

Because in front of me stands a 1987 Alfasud!

Yes, it is a car. But it is not just any car. It is beyond a classic, especially given how many have rotted their way back into the ether. There can't be that many of these still in existence, and Nigel has one here in his garage. I think of my bright red ostentatious Alfa parked not far away and I consider the similarities between Nigel and myself. I am nonplussed as I stand there, and it takes me some time to compose myself and search the rest of the garage.

Searching the rest of the garage was a bust. Aside from the car and some nice tools, there was nothing out of the ordinary in Nigel's garage. Unless, of course, you count a classic Italian coupe. I froze for a moment and then remembered that I needed to get out of there. So, I slid silently out of the garage and meandered back to my own Alfa. Once there, I sat down and checked the messages on my phone. To my surprise, I find one from Nigel which says:

What did you think of the car?

***

Right, so there is more to Nigel than meets the eye. This is not the first time he has led me on a fool's errand, and it is certainly not the first time he has gotten the better of me. Every turn I seem to make is predicted by Nigel, and I am still no closer to finding the dirt he has on me.

To make matters worse, he now knows that I am sniffing about his butt crack, and I will have to tread more carefully.

Fucking Nigel!

I say that, but I can't help but feel a sense of reverence. After all, Nigel is hiding in plain sight. He is killing bad people right in front of the police while using their resources. He has a wife, a fine taste in cars, and all told, he is doing the world a favour. I've remained at large for so long by not associating with the general public. But Nigel here goes to work every day and makes small talk about his evenings even though he has been dismembering corpses. I can't help but be a little impressed. Nigel is almost Arthur 2.0; perhaps we should be working together on this. After all, would it be so bad to have someone who understands me?

SIXTEEN.

It is Monday morning, and I am on my way to work: to work!

March has breezed its way into April, and the later evenings are filling me with renewed hope. Granted, my hope is predicated on the fact that having two sociopathic killers working together is going to make the world a better place. But I do at least feel slightly better about the situation in which I have found myself. And I allow myself a small smile as I drive.

My inner conflict is piled high in really haphazard bundles.

Nigel is a menace.

Nigel likes nice cars.

Nigel has me on the hook.

Nigel is a problem.

But at the same time, Nigel knows. Were I not indebted to him, he would probably already be dead. But, at the same time, were I not indebted to him, I might be enjoying this. I can almost imagine myself going around to his house and enjoying a cold beer while telling him all about the latest dickhead that I've killed. It would be wonderfully cathartic, and I don't know what I want anymore.

The only thing that really matters is my daughter, and not knowing much about Nigel other than where he lives, his penchant for cars, and his terrible taste in home décor, I can't trust him to leave my daughter alone. Sure, he claims to only kill bad people. But I know myself, and I know what I would be forced to do if a member of law enforcement got too close. Nigel might have a code, but I am sure that would go out of the window were his freedom in jeopardy.

I pull up at the police station and see my daughter running to her car; she is in a mild panic, and I park up and climb out of my vehicle just in time to intercept her.

'What's going on?' I ask.

'We've got a body.'

'Where?'

'Fuck it. Just get in, Dad. You're coming with.'

I shelve my thoughts and bound around to the passenger side of her Twingo. It is bright blue, and if you squint your eyes a bit, you can see that it looks a bit like a big blue flashing light—how apropos. I climb in the car and strap myself in. On the one hand, I am keen to spend time investigating crimes with my daughter; on the other, I have been getting used to the morning doughnuts that some saint brings in daily. And my dreams of tasty, sugary treats have been dashed.

Olivia gets in, and we set off at speed—the kind of speed afforded by a bright blue Twingo—and Olivia opens her mouth to speak.

'Hang on, Dad, we aren't going far.'

'Is it . . . the Hacker?' I ask diffidently.

Olivia nods.

Her car careens around a bend, and I am forced to hold on—she wasn't joking. The blue lights reflect off the mirrors and the bodywork, and I am dazzled by blue. Honestly, this isn't quite how I pictured my retirement going, but I do feel better for having dispatched Matt—it itched a dark tendency. But I don't like being on Nigel's hook, and suddenly, I'm angry again: Yes, a kill partner might be fun, but I am no one's marionette. My reverie lasts the whole car journey, and I am oblivious to my surroundings as we arrive. I don't slip back into reality until Olivia has abandoned the car at the side of the road—the way police do—and suddenly, I really am in shock.

I'm in shock because the block that stands in front of me isn't any old block of flats . . . it is mine!

***

Having composed myself, I step from the car. Olivia has long since departed, and I was starting to feel slightly self-conscious sitting in a small, vibrantly blue, French car that was ostensibly blocking a road. I feel like I am off the pace, and shit is just happening around me. A body turning up in the vicinity of my abode cannot be a coincidence, and I am going to have to fess up to the fact that I live here. Olivia has yet to frequent my new place, and a dead body in number four (I'm in six) isn't going to make that any more likely.

Having fought my way out of the small city car (and my head), I duck under the crime scene tape and show off my official consultant ID to the policewoman guarding the door. She waves me inside, but I don't get a good look at her. I'd heard the chatter on Olivia's radio, which she left in the car, that the body was in number four and I take a languid walk down the hallway to the front door. The smell hits me first, and confined dead bodies are much worse than outdoor ones. Inside are a dead couple; it is hard to make out their features because, once again, their brains have been removed from their skulls. The pair lie side-by-side on the floor, and their brains are missing altogether. I exhale and look slightly deeper; from the ligature marks on their wrists, I can see that both were bound at one point, which is beyond a joke. This is the handiwork of my new best friend, and if I wasn't angry before, I am now.

'It looks like this was done while they were still alive!' I hear the voice before I see the dickhead to whom it belongs, and before long, I feel the weight of someone's hand on my shoulder.

I turn about to see Nigel, who must have sauntered into the room, sporting a simper, and I make sure that my turning about shrugs my shoulder free from his awkward embrace. But Nigel's hand grapples with my shoulder, and it lingers there. I reach into my pocket and find a ballpoint pen that resides in there. I extend the point of the pen and slowly lift it from my pocket.

'Hi Nigel,' I say as politely as possible. The pen comes free from my pocket, and I hide it in the palm of my hand. I raise my hand in the direction of Nigel's head, but we are interrupted by the presence of Olivia as she re-enters the room from somewhere else.

'Ah, my two favourite guys,' she says as cheerfully as possible. 'Is it him?' she asks, addressing Nigel.

'I've just got here, but I'd say yes, from the looks of it. I was telling Arthur here that based on the previous body, the dismemberment is taking place while these people are alive.'

I pat Nigel on the arm and then lower my hand back to my pocket. I was close to ending him here and now. I've killed with a pen before, and Nigel was close to finding out how it's really done.

'Do we know anything about them?'

'Duncan Harvey and his girlfriend Belinda. We suspect that they were tied up in human trafficking, but we've never been able to prove it.'

I nod. It fits, and from Nigel's happy demeanour, I can tell it is him. They say that these people like to return to the scene of the crime, and he is getting his gratification every time a murder is called in. Nigel gets to relive the scene and gets paid for it every time he is called out. And one thing is certain: Nigel is doing this for the kicks as much as anything else.

It also doesn't take a rocket scientist to figure out why Nigel has chosen to kill some of my neighbours—I will face scrutiny for this. He is taunting me, showing me just how close he can get to my life without completely ruining it. And now I'm certain that we are not friends. Winnie the Pooh would never do this to Eeyore, and I'm on a fast track to the 'Anti-Nigel Club'.

Confessing to my peers that my flat was just down the hallway was met with both suspicion and sympathy. Which is an odd mix of human emotions to take in. The suspicion, I garnered, was nothing personal. The police are a naturally suspicious bunch. Regardless, as sorry as they were for my plight (and my residence becoming a crime scene), I was forced to answer some questions at the station.

Having been questioned, I was free to go. But I don't like this situation at all. I was close to killing Nigel in a room surrounded by police officers. He has me wound up, I'm questioning myself and I am riddled with doubt. I want to be able to confide in someone, but there is only Nigel for this, and I'm sure that telling him I am grappling with whether, how and when I should kill him will probably not go down that well. I miss Ophelia. I miss being known through and through, and I'm certain that deep down, I will be alone forever.

Some might say that I deserve it, but I never asked for this. I do my best with the cards I was dealt, that is all.

With all that is going on in my head, I hop in the car and take a drive. I don't know where I am going, but 505 primed

Italian horses take the strain from my brain, and I settle back and enjoy the drive.

And I don't know how it happened! I don't. There I was, taking a nice leisurely drive to nowhere, and the next thing I knew, I was pulling up somewhere awful. Somewhere soul-destroying-ly horrific. I entered a place worse than Hell.

Judy's!

To say that Judy was less than impressed to see me on a weekday evening was an understatement. But given that I had made the drive from Southampton up to London, she had little choice but to let me in. After all, I'll have to pay the congestion and ULEZ charge—twice.

Judy let me in, and before I knew it, I was sitting on a recliner in her stately London penthouse with a cold beer in my hand. It almost felt normal.

'What do you want, Arthur?' is the first thing Judy says to me. I rise from my recliner and move towards the window.

'Is that The Shard?' I ask in disbelief.

'What do you want, Arthur? I had plans this evening, you know.'

'What plans could you have?'

Judy shoots me a look, and suddenly, I'm sorry I asked.

'Ew, gross.'

'Maybe you should think about sex, too, Arthur. It might save you driving to mine on a weekday evening.'

'I need help, Judy. And please, I don't want to think about you . . . you know.'

'What did you say?'

'I need help.'

'Strange, I thought that was what you said. Who have you killed this time? I told you, Arthur, I can't keep clearing up your mess—'

'It concerns Olivia.'

'What have you done?'

'Me?' I ask.

'Yes, Arthur. You—'

'It's the Hampshire Hacker; she works with him!'

'You what?' Judy nearly leaps out of her chair. Having unsettled herself, Judy walks over to the side, pours herself a drink from a large decanter, and then sits back down, taking a large sip.

'Go on.'

'Nigel.'

'And that explains it, does it?'

I shake my head.

'A forensic pathologist that she works with, he goes by the name of Nigel, and he's killing—'

'Can't you, you know . . .'

I shake my head. It is weird that when it comes to our family, Judy is down with killing. Granted, Nigel deserves it, but still.

'Why not?'

'It's, er, complicated.'

'What have you done?'

'Nigel might have lured me into a trap!'

'For fuck's sake, Arthur.'

Hearing Saint Judy swear throws me off for a second. I knew she wouldn't understand, but there aren't any other options for people to talk to.

'Look, Judy, let's not get bogged down by the details; Nigel is a danger and if I, you know, then he will leak sensitive information about me. I just want to keep my daughter safe.'

Judy nods, and I think when it comes to family, she understands. She went to some lengths to keep me out of jail, and she doesn't like me. I do not doubt that she will go to the end of the Earth for her niece.

'Give me everything you have on him.'

I nod. 'Will do.' I stand and motion to leave, but Judy also stands and blocks my path.

'You're not driving home after drinking,' she says. And I realise that, for a change, she is drinking, too.

'And you certainly aren't driving my car after beer.' I go to tell her that her car has been sitting idly outside my house, but I don't think it is quite the time for it.

'You can sleep here,' she says. 'But you'll need to leave when I leave, and I get up early.'

I nod. It will be a nice change of pace to spend the night away from home and all my troubles. I settle down in my chair, and before I know it, Judy has poured herself another drink and one for me, too.

She sits back down and says, 'So tell me everything about Nigel . . .'

SEVENTEEN.

Baring my soul to Judy was painful. Getting kicked out by her at six-thirty a.m. was even more so. Still, it does feel good to unburden myself, and knowing Judy's powers, it is also pleasing to know that she is working away in the shadows, digging into Nigel.

The drive back to mine was simple until I hit the M3 motorway (as-per-fucking-usual), and it took me over three hours to get back home. I pulled up, parked up and then took the wander over the small road that separates the car park and the flats. And I am almost in a good mood. I open the door to the communal area and walk down the corridor towards my flat. I take a left at the end, and my mood instantly plummets.

It plummets, because, sitting outside my door on the floor is Nigel!

'He looks up at me from the ground and says: 'The traffic must have been murder!'

Okay, so Nigel seems to know exactly what I'm up to! He also appears to be one step ahead of me at every turn.

And to make matters worse, we are sitting in his Vauxhall Corsa, with our knives, on our way to murder Alan—so much for it being my choice! It's a Vauxhall Corsa, too. It's even the 'limited edition'—limited as long as you don't include the other four hundred thousand of them! Is there a worse car out there?

'Are you excited?' asks Nigel as he breaks my reverie. 'I'm excited.'

I nod.

I am not excited. I am far, far, far from excited. This is bad. Not only is Nigel a lunatic, but he's an organised one— a very tidy, organised lunatic.

And I know I am not one to judge anyone's mental state. But Nigel does need to be tucked up in a nice secure home . . . for the criminally insane.

Nigel's Corsa bumbles along a country lane, and it is then that I notice we are somewhere near Botley.

'What are we doing out here?' I ask.

'Alan likes to train spot; he should be out here today in a nice quiet patch. Come on, Arthur, we have to catch him somewhere nice and secluded where we can have a little chat.'

I nod along to Nigel and then fall back into my head. I'll be honest; I'd rather be sitting next to a box of very suspect hand grenades than Nigel. But we do what we can with what we have.

'Any particular body part you want?'

'What?'

'You're going to have to call dibs.'

'You what?'

I turn to look at Nigel, and he grins at me. His face is a picture, and he might be salivating.

'It's your day out,' he continues, 'if you want the head, you're going to have to call it.'

I look at Nigel, almost in disbelief. Is this really what some of us are like?

'I'm not that bothered,' I reply.

'Suit yourself,' says Nigel. 'But don't say I didn't warn you. You'll only be disappointed in yourself.'

I slip back into my head and wonder how on earth I can be disappointed for not bagsying Alan's head. The ride continues in silence for a few moments, and before I know it, we are pulling up in a small car park. Nigel parks the car, puts it in neutral and then kills the engine. Silence falls in the car as the engine stops, and it is almost chunky enough to eat.

'We've got to be a team on this,' says Nigel.

'I—'

'I know. I know. You're the GOAT. But hear me out: we have to be on the same page. If Alan gets away, we are both in hot water.'

Short of a better plan, I nod.

'He'll be on a small train bridge over there looking out through his binoculars. As long as he's alone, we'll surprise him, drag him to the woods, and do our thing. Just follow my lead.'

I nod once more and then consider the use of the phrase *do our thing*! Is that really how Nigel does it? Just by doing his thing? This guy has been leading the police on a merry chase for months now, and his process is to grab a man from a bridge, in broad daylight, and then *do his thing*.

I acquiesce to Nigel's demands, and we step from the car. The April sun hits me on the face and reminds me that we are actually doing this. I am about to kill Alan from Harry Ramsden's with Nigel from work because Nigel said so! Is this really what I have become? This is egregious. My anger rises slightly as I step from the vehicle, and it isn't long before I am halted in my tracks by Nigel's constant yapping.

'Don't forget your knives!'

I turn and look back at Nigel, who is digging a large set of knives and a backpack out of the car. He looks like he is about to take a hike before competing on MasterChef, and this whole thing is insane. The notion hits me that I might be caught attempting to hack a man to pieces in the woods with Nigel from work, and I am disgusted. Maybe this is why serial killers keep to themselves. The only people who can understand the real them are deranged psychopaths who think they are the real-life version of Arrow—or at least Arrow until it went south.

I take a step back towards the car, grab my leather knife pouch from the boot, and slide it under my arm before Nigel closes it.

And now here we are. Alan is in our sights, and he is just staring away at trains, that aren't there, through his binoculars. Nigel reaches into his bag, removes a rag and a bottle of chloroform—old school—and proceeds to douse the rag with the chemical. The perks of being a lunatic pathologist, I guess. With the rag sufficiently doused, Nigel lowers his belongings to the ground, checks that the coast is clear and then, putting his finger to his lip (as if I wasn't aware that I should remain quiet), he raises himself from the bush we are lurking behind and goes after Alan.

I watch on, spellbound, as it all unfolds in front of me. Alan gets a hint that someone is behind him and slowly lowers the binoculars from his eyes, but he is far too slow. Nigel is on him like a panther on the attack—and he is fast, I'll give him that—Nigel wraps the drug-covered rag around Alan's face, and there is a mild scuffle before Nigel is holding Alan's limp body in his hands. Then he looks over to me and beckons me out of my hiding place with his head. I am not a fan of being summoned, and I stand my ground until Nigel says:

'Are you going to help me, or what?'

I raise my ageing frame from behind the bush, check the coast is clear, and then amble over to Nigel. Once there, we take Alan between us and sort of drape him over our shoulders like a drunken friend. Then, once Alan is in place, we return to our belongings, grab them, and begin to drag Alan out into the woods.

Dragging a full-grown man into the woods is not an easy task! I can see why Nigel wanted my help. That aside, I am still not happy to be here, and I am questioning where I went wrong in life.

Having dragged old Al out into the woods, we set about taping him to a tree—not sustainable—and now we are waiting for him to regain consciousness.

Again, I can see why Nigel wanted company; there is nothing to do when you are trapped in a vacancy.

When Alan finally regains consciousness, he is firmly taped to a tree. He thrashes about momentarily until he realises that it is futile. There is a look in his eye; it is a mixture of *fuck*, mixed in with, *oh shit, I've been caught*. No one ever expects their years of malfeasance and general bellendry to catch up with them. But Alan's eyes do scream 'guilty', and I do at least feel slightly better about what we are about to do. I look deep into Alan's guilty eyes, and they shout at me, well, they would if they could. I can see the fear as it flickers in them, and I don't feel good about killing a man who is taped to a tree.

Nigel, who has been oddly quiet, then pipes up.

'Cut off his head!'

I look at Nigel as though he just asked me to ram one of my fingers up him and say:

'Come again?'

'Cut off his head.'

Okay, so Nigel is insane. I have a set of knives with me, and they are good, but cutting off a man's head while he is still alive and trying to kick is more than excessive. I am wearing an old shirt, but I still don't want it to be covered in blood, which will happen. And I'm wearing my hiking boots, and I really, really don't want them to fill up with Alan's blood.

Nigel reaches into his knife carrier and removes a big, jagged blade. Once out, he holds it out to me and says:

'Cut off his head.'

I feel like I'm in eighteenth-century France. The words *cut off his head* have been said so many times, and I'm feeling queasy and starting to get angry. Nigel is resolute and the blade in his outstretched hand doesn't even begin to quiver.

'Did I stutter?' he asks.

I'm going to be honest; I'm starting to dislike Nigel. I thought this might be fun. I thought Nigel might understand me. But I think I have more in common with a cement mixer than I do with Nigel here, and his issuing of orders is pissing me off.

'Cut off his head!' The knife in Nigel's hand starts to waver, and, finally, I take it from his hand and wrap my hand around the handle. I take a step towards Alan and mouth the words *I'm sorry*. Granted, it doesn't make up for the fact that you were having a nice day, out spotting trains and then you woke up and your head is about to be hacked off. But it is the best I can do. I stop just short of Alan, and the tears are streaming from his eyes now. His mouth is firmly taped together, but I can see him trying to move his mouth.

'Do it, or I'll release the photos. I'm not sure what your daughter will make of you once she finds out—'

Nigel's words are abruptly halted by me turning and jabbing the knife into his neck. He coughs, he splutters, and he gurgles. Blood then begins to cascade out of his neck like a bloody Angel Falls, and it isn't long before he slumps to his knees and grabs at his neck in futility.

Okay, so this is very problematic. I didn't plan this through, and I didn't like how Nigel was speaking to me. I have just killed one of the Hampshire Hackers with a witness present, and I have no idea what to do next.

In my defence, Nigel was fucking mental. But that doesn't help me out of my current situation.

Alan is still taped to the tree, and he's definitely pissed himself. There might be a small, or a large douche, too. I can't say for sure. What is certain, though, is Alan is fucking petrified—which is fair—if I actually felt anything, I might be scared too.

But I'm not.

The world needed Nigel gone. And now he is. There is the small matter of his evidence on me and the fact that Alan here has just watched me kill a man in cold blood. Granted, I have just saved his life, but we did kidnap him and threaten to cut off his head. I look at Nigel's bloody body on the floor, and I'm fucking glad that he's stopped talking. Nigel was starting to irritate me, and now that he's gone, I realise that he had an annoying, tinny voice. It was like a speaker with one broken wire; it made noise but didn't sound right.

I switch my gaze from Nigel to Alan. He is still taped to the tree (obviously), and he is still pissing. Seriously, Alan, how much piss do you even have?

My eyes buzz back and forth between Alan and dead Nigel like a metronome. Honestly, I didn't think this through, and I don't know what to do with Nigel's body or with Alan. The obvious answer would be to get Alan to help me with Nigel's body, but then I don't know what to do with Alan. On the one hand, he's a menace (yet to be fully proved), but on the other, I don't know if I can just kill him. I'm supposed to be different to these monsters. With the knife (I used to kill Nigel) still in my hand, I turn towards Alan and waggle the knife in his face menacingly. Alan gets my gist, and I tell him that *I will untie him, and as long as he does what he's told, he will live to see another day.* Alan nods, and I cut away at the ties that bind. As soon as he is free, Alan steps towards me and throws his arms around me in a hug. Now, I'm not the biggest fan of hugs at the best of times, and Alan here has just pissed himself. So, it's safe to say that I would rather be dangling my private parts in an alligator-filled swamp than be here hugging Alan. But I do need his help.

The first thing I have Alan do is remove all of the tape from the tree (sorry, tree), and then we set about moving Nigel's body. Options are limited, so I employ Alan, and we carry Nigel's body over to the train bridge.

Now, I should admit: the poor train driver who unwittingly mows over Nigel's body is probably going to be scarred for life. But Nigel is already dead, and having his body hacked to pieces by a moving train is a very effective way of getting rid of it, especially when it will be made to look as though the Hampshire Hacker finally felt some guilt at what he had done and took his own life.

'Thank you,' says Alan as we walk Nigel's body back to the train bridge. I go to smile at Alan, but a nettle catches me between my sock and my shoe, and it wipes away any would-be smiles. As pain distracts me from Alan's grin, I take a moment to study him. Alan is dark-haired and balding. The hair is still there, but it is clearly in decline. His face features the familiar scars of teenage acne. He is wearing a striped t-shirt that fits badly and a pair of piss-soaked jeans. We arrive back at the bridge, and Alan has come full circle. We set

Nigel's body down and take a breath. Despite not being at a full complement of blood, Nigel's body still weighs a ton, and we catch our breaths in an awkward silence. To say that I didn't think I'd be disposing of Nigel's body with Alan the menace today would be an understatement.

After re-filling our lungs, we bend down, and then on three, we throw Nigel's body over the edge. It lands on the tracks with a sickening *thud* and even I am forced to wince. Alan stares at the track longingly, and I can see that, for him, the opportunity to spot a train running over a corpse is like all of his fantasies mixed into one, and piss pants or not, I'm fairly sure he is salivating at the mouth. I take a good look at Alan as he stares longingly at the track, and although Nigel was a lunatic, he certainly seems to have been correct about Alan.

Alan.

Alan.

Fucking Alan.

My mind is working overdrive as I watch a giddy Alan as he watches a train approaching in the distance. I honestly don't know what to do. I should rid the world of Alan, but if I kill him, I am back to square one (minus Alan's help because he'll be dead), and I can't very well have Alan take the jump along with Nigel. Can I?

With Alan's attention firmly focused on the impending train, I remove the knife, which I had stashed under my belt, and I sneak up behind Alan. The man is too fixated by trains to notice me, and I grab him from behind and raise the knife to his throat.

'Tell anyone about this, and I'll kill you.'

He nods.

'I know where you live, where you work, and where you eat. I will be watching you.'

Alan nods frenetically, and suddenly, I hear waterworks again. Seriously, Alan? I take a step back, lest I get covered in Alan's piss, and retreat from the scene. Alan remains glued to the spot, and I walk backwards until I make it to the path. Safely back at the footpath, I turn about and head back to Nigel's car. I hear the train coming in the distance, and I grin. What a weird day today has been!

EIGHTEEN.

I wake up and sit bolt-upright in bed. It is now Friday, and April is on a fast march towards May.

To say it has been a weird few weeks would be an understatement. It's been three days since I killed Nigel, and so far, nothing has happened. I should be more alarmed. But there isn't much I can do.

Nigel's death made the regional news. I say that. A death made the news. Nigel's body has yet to be identified—given that all that was left were a few remains. But it will be in time, and Nigel's absence is starting to be noticed in the department. I don't know what I'm doing.

Alan has seen my face and is a witness to me killing Nigel. I need to do something about Alan, but the truth is, all I know about him is where he works.

There is also the small (rather large) matter of what Nigel has on me and where, and I do wake up every morning expecting to be staring down the barrel. But it hasn't happened yet, which means time is still on my side. Since I can only face one problem at a time, today, my focus will be on Alan.

Deal with Alan.

Find Nigel's dirt.

Frame Nigel as the Hampshire Hacker.

And when did life become so complicated? In France, I had to deal with the small local supermarket . . . and the locals in general. But that was my biggest problem. Ever since I've been back, I've been faced with one issue after another. My time is supposed to be spent with my daughter, but instead, I seem to be hanging out with a who's who of Hampshire serial murderers . . . and is this my club?

I climb out of my bed and look at my telephone; there are myriad missed calls, and I do feel a slight pang of guilt at having returned to everyone's lives only to be wholly absent. I should be seeing my friends, my daughter, and, dare I say it, my family. Instead, I am chasing a ticking clock. Surely, Nigel had some sort of dead man switch in place, and it cannot be long before the truth about me comes out. I need to check in on Alan. I need to find Nigel's dirt. And most pressingly, I need to reply to about fifty missed WhatsApp messages.

I'm not a fan of group chats. It is safe to say that I would rather deliberately give myself frostbite than be in a group chat. But when you have a group of friends, these things happen, like it or not. The problem is, when you miss a few hours of chat, you miss hundreds of messages, too. I exhale, I pull my phone close to my eyes—so that I can read it—and I begin to deal with the myriad messages.

Having dealt with the messages, I shit, shower, shave, and then prepare myself for the day ahead. I am still officially a police consultant, but Nigel's disappearance has everyone at the station worried, and everything has turned horribly mawkish.

Oh, where's Nigel?

I do hope Nigel is okay!

Poor Nigel!

Where's Nigel?

Hopefully, he's rotting in the depths of Hell, with his tinny voice and his predilection for chopping off live heads. Nigel was a Horrible Hampshire Hacker, and he should not be missed at all.

And yet he is.

The police station is losing their collective mind that one of their own is missing.

I dress and then mooch my way out to the car. I don't like that the spotlight is on Nigel, and my drive is mundane.

I arrive at the police station to find a rather large collective huddle. It appears that everyone is gathered in the lobby, and there is a lot of chatter. I push my way through the throngs of people and find my daughter somewhere near the front of the crowd. There are tears in those beautiful eyes of hers, and suddenly, I am upset and anxious at the same time.

She sees me and instantly places her head on my shoulder.

'Oh, Dad,' she says. And she sobs for what seems like an eternity before she says: 'It's Nigel!'

My ears prick up at the sound of that prick, and suddenly, I am very much paying attention.

'What about him?' I ask as innocently as possible. Knowing full well that Nigel is currently in as many bits as the rest of the police population.

'This guy, erm, Alan, something. He says that he saw the Hampshire Hacker throw Nigel over a train bridge. He gave us the location, and we are working on a DNA sample from a recent John Doe we found. Dad, it looks like it's going to be him. I don't know what to do!'

I don't know what to do, either. I grab Olivia by the shoulders and pull her in close to me. Everything is spiralling out of control, and suddenly, I'm pissed off that I let Alan live. The little weasel has played his hand, presumably to let me know that he, too, has dirt on me. He is playing a very dangerous game given his potential nefarious behaviour, and he has put himself firmly in my crosshairs. . .

. . . Not that I can kill a police witness without raising yet more concerns. I just have to hope that Alan keeps his mouth shut.

The initial shock eventually dies down, and the assembled crowd is called back to work. The day moves on as planned (eventually), and by five o'clock, I am finally free to sneak about the place unmolested.

Alan is still in an interview room, but I see that he is alone, and I slide inside and shut the door behind me. Alan's eyes meet mine, and there is a flash of panic. He looks about the room and then remembers that he is in a police station—safe ground. Neither of us can act here.

Having turned off the recording equipment, I slide into the chair opposite Alan, compose myself, and then say, 'You're playing a dangerous game.'

Alan simpers and then says:

'So are you.'

'What do you want?' I almost hiss at him. The words slither sibilantly from my lips to his ears, and when they arrive, he grins before opening his mouth.

'I want to work together!'

The words hit my ears, and I slump my head back against the chair. We've gone full circle, and I was afraid that it would come to this. I've managed to rid myself of one lunatic partner, and in comes another one, bright-eyed and bushy-tailed. And I couldn't have written this. It is like my life is the elaborate plot of someone's story; if I'm honest, I'm not in the mood for this.

But I am aware that Alan knows. He knows that there is more to me than meets the eye, and he did witness me thrust a knife into Nigel's neck. Nigel was a twat. But he was also part of the police force. If Alan blabs, I will feel the full weight of the police coming down upon me, and my freedom of movement will be restricted for some time. Granted, it is just Alan's word against mine. But being implicated in a murder—for the second time—really wouldn't be a good look for me. I also may well get incarcerated for a period of time, during which Nigel's photo of me breaking Matt's neck may well surface . . . which would rather compound my problems. I need to placate Alan. I need to keep him where I can see him.

'Fine,' I say. 'But we do exactly what I say and when.'

Alan grins. It seems that he got all the pissing out of his system, and he composes himself. Alan stretches his hand out towards me, and I don't want to shake it.

But, short of a better plan, I grab Alan's outstretched arm, and our hands meet. His is moist and clammy, like a damp sponge.

It looks as though I have a new, rather pissy partner.

NINETEEN.

Alan pissed me off!

I had wanted to frame Nigel as the Hampshire Hacker . . . given that he sort of was. But now, Nigel will simply be poor Nigel, which is not what I wanted. No sympathy should be bestowed upon the shoulders of that lunatic. Nigel got off lightly for his crimes, and I'm still not happy that he has tarnished my legacy. I don't want to go down in the same history as Nigel, and I need to do something about Alan!

Alan wouldn't give me his address—sensible—so I gave him mine and then immediately looked up Alan's in the police paperwork. It would seem Alan isn't the brightest of the bunch, which only serves to fuel my ire.

And why is this all happening to me? It would seem that every week someone new finds out all of my dirty secrets and I am starting to prefer the days that I wallowed on my own. None of this happened in France, or dare I say it, during my great depression following Melissa's death.

But enough about Alan. He is on side and keeping his mouth shut, which means that for the time being I can focus on the present: Nigel's funeral!

I'm not entirely sure what the etiquette is regarding attending funerals that you caused. This is a first for me, and I'm not sure how I feel. Nigel was deserving of death, that's for sure, but I now have to mingle with the family of the dearly departed, knowing full well that it was me who made him depart!

I rise from my chair as I battle my reverie. My mind takes over, and the next thing I know, I am in a taxi on my way to Nigel's funeral.

The service for Nigel takes place at Southampton Crematorium, which I secretly hope isn't what he wanted.

The crematorium is basic—no offence, Southampton Crematorium—and looks as much like every other crematorium as possible. It is bland. It is dated. And my god, couldn't someone have made crematoriums at least slightly cheery? Anything to do with life features playful cartoons and bubbles, but when it comes to death, we like everything to be as dull as possible.

My taxi arrives outside West Chapel, and I thank the driver for his limited small talk and depart the vehicle. I could have met with Olivia, but she was riding with Nigel's family, and I didn't think that was quite okay.

Hi, I'm your son's killer. He was deeply unhinged. Oh, and by the way, he killed scores of people.

Small talk isn't my best attribute.

I keep to myself as I take the short walk to the building and step inside. I find my seat and take a pew. Before long, Olivia appears and sits next to me. Her presence calms me, and she places her hand over mine. I turn to her and look into her eyes. The service starts, and I dip inside my head. My reverie jumps into full swing and before I know it, we are standing motionless at the wake.

'I'll get us some drinks,' I say. Olivia smiles at me, and I depart. I shuffle my way across to the bar and try to catch the bartender's attention. I am minding my own business when a female appears in my periphery and sidles up to me. I turn to see a familiar figure and it takes me all of thirty seconds to realise who it is: Grace!

'Grace, hi,' I manage.

I'm not sure that *hi* cuts it.

Hi, I killed your husband.

Hi, your life has been shattered because of me.

Hi . . .

Grace looks me up and down, reaches into her bag, and removes a small envelope.

'Nigel, *sniff,* wanted you to have this.' She dabs at her eyes with a small tissue she produced from nowhere and then departs as quickly as she arrived. I'm no rocket scientist, but one look at the envelope tells me everything I need to know. I question, for a moment, whether Grace is involved in this. But I get the feeling that if she knew that her husband was both murdered and a murderer, she might not be so calm right now. I pocket the envelope and shudder. Then I go back in search of my daughter.

The rest of the wake moved on, and Nigel was sufficiently 'toasted'. It feels a tad unfair that he will not go down in history as the maniac he was, but I have very little to go on, and convincing the world that Nigel was, in fact, the Hampshire Hacker is very low on my list of priorities right now. Before I know it, my taxi is dropping me off at my flat and I'm alone.

Being alone is as great as it is terrible. My thoughts spin wildly out of control, and taming them is like trying to ride a rodeo bull . . . that's on fire. There are so many things going on right now, and I don't know where to start. My excitement at being back has been dashed by the many serial killers who seem to want to frequent my life. I know it is a cliché, but we are supposed to be loners . . . and when did this get so complicated? I'm still unhappy with the 'club' I've found myself in and don't know what to do. Alan has bought himself a position of safety, and holy-fucking-shit! Nigel's wife, Grace, handed me an envelope at the wake.

I remove the envelope from my pocket with care and take a seat on the sofa opposite the TV. My flat is calm and quiet, but on the inside, I am all noise. The envelope is sealed, but it can only contain one thing. I close my eyes and slide my fingers under the seal. Whatever Nigel's saliva contained, it was horrendously sticky, and the envelope is sealed with vigour. Failing to get my finger into the flaps, I rip open the top and pour the contents out onto my lap. The first thing I see is glitter—fucking glitter—and then out slides the rather predictable photo . . . only the photo is not quite what I expected. It's a tough one to explain. The scene has a careful composition. There is a box and a mobile phone; the phone sits next to the box, and the box has a photo—of me killing Matt—propped up next to it. In the background, I can make out some depressingly drab décor and it just has to be somewhere in the police station. I turn the picture over and written on the back, in wonderful cursive, are the words: *tick tock!* and that's it.

I place the photo on my lap and stare into space. Nigel has hidden his dirt somewhere in the police station. The phone is probably traceable, and I'm sure that will come into play at some point. So, I have as long as it takes before someone, presumably Grace, realises that Nigel has a second phone and has the police track it. Nigel, being Nigel, will have made that happen before the battery on the phone dies. Meaning I am very much on the clock.

Fucking Nigel.

And I'm sure the glitter isn't sustainable. This whole thing is so elaborate, and I knew I didn't like Nigel. The phone in the picture is a Nokia 3310 (known for its battery prowess), and it looks like I'm going to the police station.

I'll be honest: playing high-stakes hide and seek wasn't what I had planned for this evening. The desk sergeant let me in— under the guise of collecting some of my belongings—and now I am in the station. I have no idea where Nigel might have hidden my evidence; I have the photo for reference, but it is a big, drab building, and it could literally be anywhere.

This is dreadful! I can't believe I was even considering being friends with Nigel. I feel like I'm in the bad plot of Die Hard Nine, and I don't know how it came to this. I am being blackmailed from beyond the grave, and how is this my life? Finding the box and phone might solve all of my problems, but who is to say that was Nigel's only contingency? He might well have been a maniac, but Nigel sure was organised.

The police station at night is not a place I want to be. It is full of ghosts of criminals past, and it is too far away from Christmas to be making these kinds of connections. My time should be spent with my daughter and not on some scavenger hunt at Southampton police station. On the upside, my brain is certainly occupied, but I could be spending my time more productively. I could be seeing my daughter, or even Judy, for that matter. I could be swinging golf clubs with Rich Richard. Not drinking wine with Abdul or avoiding undue sentiment with my parents. But no! Here I am, chasing a ghost around a police station.

Time ticks away as I frantically hunt high and low. I have no idea where I am looking, and before long, I find myself in the morgue.

The morgue is a strange place on your own. It is even stranger when you were directly responsible for killing its resident pathologist. I can smell Nigel everywhere and I'm not happy that Alan bore witness to me dispatching him.

Alan is a problem.

But so are phones that might be discovered.

My reverie breaks as a phone rings and shakes me from my thoughts. Alas, it is not a mobile, and my search continues. Surely, Nigel's office would be too easy, but I enter it anyway and sit down.

If I were Nigel, where would I hide a phone. . . ?

I wriggle my butt in Nigel's chair and pause to think. On Nigel's desk is a Rolodex, and I begin to leaf through it absent-mindedly. Serendipity finds me just when I need it most, as the second entry I come across is labelled 'burner'. I reach into my pocket, remove my phone and then begin to dial the 11 numbers in front of me. A phone rings in the next room, and I am out of my chair and on the move before I know what is happening. I move into a storeroom and locate the ringing phone. It is sitting on a shelf just above head height, and I grab it along with an accompanying box. I bring both down and switch off the phone before removing the SIM card and snapping it in half. The back of the shelf matches the photo, and I am certain that this is the box. I reach into the box and remove yet another piece of paper.

The second piece of paper is for a parcel tracking number sent with Royal Mail, and Nigel is fucking with me from beyond the grave.

I waste no time typing the tracking number into Royal Mail's website, and the information that it returns is very unpleasant. It is unpleasant because it would appear that the package is due at my daughter's house in just over 24 hours!

A scavenger hunt! Cheers, Nigel. You fucking dick!

Being in your mid-60s is bad for your health in general. I am closer to death than I have ever been, and cigarette smoke is starting to make me feel queasy. It has been years since I saw a doctor and even longer since I saw a dentist. The former being a problem. My heart rate is through the roof, and I can feel my blood pressure rising. My health is not something I have ever really cared much about, but I am starting to feel laggy. The pressures of being a father, being a member of the new raving lunatic party, as well as having a dead psychopath with a stranglehold on me are starting to tell.

I don't have time to see a doctor, but a strange sensation in my chest tells me otherwise. Plus, if you don't make time for your wellness, you are making time for your illness. So, with a heavy heart (quite literally), I dig into my pocket and ring my GP . . . or at least I would . . .

. . . But gone are the days when one can simply phone a doctor and make an appointment. No. That would be simple. What you have to do instead is go online. Go online, fill in a form and then wait! Wait. You have to wait. What if I am dying? What then?

Despite the lack of urgency involved in reporting my illness. I fill in the form . . . tap . . . tap . . . tap. Enter my symptoms . . . tap . . . tap . . . tap. Heavy heart. Feeling breathless, etc. And then I press send.

And then I wait.

But all I have is time. The package will be delivered to my daughter tomorrow (hopefully when she is out), and there isn't much I can do in between. And, short of a better plan, I go around to see my daughter.

And much to my surprise, Abdul and Maureen are already in attendance.

'Hi Abdul. Hi Maureen,' I say as I enter the living room and sit down. To say that today has been a whirlwind would be a dramatic understatement, but it really has passed me by.

But Maureen being here is to my advantage.

Maureen is probably the most intense person I know. But she is a surgeon, and surgeons do have to go through medical school before they begin to dice people up for a living.

'It sounds like high blood pressure to me,' says Maureen. 'Maybe just the flu. It's not that big a deal for someone of your age!'

Not that big a deal?

I feel like I'm suffocating in my own body, and that's not a big deal.

'Have you made a doctor's appointment?' asks Abdul.

'Yeah, Dad,' chimes in Olivia, 'you should see someone about that.'

I roll my eyes as I recall my trials and tribulations (that were a small part of the day), and I sigh. The conversation moves on, and before I know it, Abdul and Maureen are on their way home.

Now, I should admit I have made no plans to stay here. But I need to stay here. I need to be here for when Nigel's nefarious note arrives. I need to know what is in the package and, presumably, move on to my next clue. I know I've said it, but Nigel is a cunt. Imagine making me work hard for this?

Olivia invites me to stay over (she has plenty of guest bedrooms) and my plan is working. I move from the living room, up the stairs and into the spare room. I have completed my ablutions before I really know what is happening, and finally, I set myself down in bed.

The day has thoroughly passed me by, and it isn't long before my eyes are closed, and I am fast asleep.

I awake early the next day and almost jump from my bed. This is the United Kingdom. Despite having the same routes, post can be delivered anytime between eight and three. The package is to be delivered before one p.m., and I need to be here, and Olivia doesn't. I look at my watch in a blind panic and see that I overslept. It is just gone eight a.m., and I really should have set an alarm.

I plough downstairs and see my daughter donning her coat ready for work.

'Morning, Rip Van Winkel,' she says. 'I'm just heading to work; you want to come with?'

I shake my head vehemently.

'No,' I say curtly. 'I still need to shower.'

'Very well,' says Olivia. She moves towards the stairs, raises herself onto her tiptoes and then kisses me on the cheek. 'I'll see you later then?'

And like that, she is gone.

And I'm just glad that Nigel's letter didn't arrive before I woke. I do feel slightly bad sneaking about my daughter like this. But what's the alternative?

Sorry, I killed Nigel because he was a complete psychopath. I'm also the original Hampshire Hacker, and I've been killing people since before you were born. Can I have a hug?

You see? It doesn't quite work.

Fortunately, my plan of 'camp out at my daughter's house' worked. And Nigel's letter was delivered, on time, by Royal Mail—which is a pleasant surprise.

The letter itself was no surprise. Nigel's scavenger hunt continues. Only this time, there is no clue. Just the threat that the information will be delivered to my daughter in two weeks!

It's weird because Nigel was very organised. He knew this letter would find its way to me, and he's given me time. I have two weeks to solve this, or my daughter will find out what I do in a very visceral way. The image of me snapping Matt's neck will find its way to her, and I am almost powerless to stop it.

On one hand, this is insidious. My true self is going to be exposed to my daughter. On the other, I have been running about like a madman trying to stop this from happening. The news that I have two weeks is somewhat comforting and does allow me to relax for a while. But knowing Nigel, there is going to be almost no way that I stop this information from reaching my daughter. The letter reads as follows:

Dear Arthur,

I had wanted to work together. Think of all the good the two of us could have done. Think of what we might have achieved. Old and new, brothers in arms.

If you're reading this, I am dead, and you have been very vigilant so far. But since my time has come to an end, so will yours. You have two weeks to get your affairs in order. Two weeks until your daughter finds out who you are.

Do the words come from my lips or yours?

Tick-tock, Arthur.

It's not signed by anyone, but I can only assume that it is Nigel who has sent me this letter. And I'll be honest, I have no idea how someone even goes about arranging all of this from beyond the grave; it is impressive. Knowing that I have time does salve my wounded pride at having been bested by Nigel. But the reality is, unless I can stop this from happening, I have two weeks to decide whether I tell my daughter about myself. If not, Nigel does. And I don't want that. Plus, if I explain it, she might understand. Maybe she'll accept me and my dark tendencies. Maybe she won't. But one thing is for sure . . . it looks like she is going to find out.

And since there is nothing to do when you are stuck in a vacancy. I may as well enjoy my time.

I suppose Nigel has done me a favour. I don't know how he will do it, but he will tell my daughter—something I've been wrestling with for some time. I need to feel known. And

I need to know that someone understands me. The fear of being alone among people has overwhelmed me, and I need to end it.

So . . . with two weeks to kill, I shelve my plans, pack up and leave my daughter's and then head home.

TWENTY.

Day one of my two weeks: I am at the doctor. And the prognosis isn't good. The good news is that I don't have high blood pressure. The bad news is that it's probably my lungs. I have been a smoker for thirty-odd years . . . all those warning labels.

'So, what now?' I ask the doctor more out of hope than anything else.

Having examined me, the tall, balding man sits back down in his chair and begins to tap away at his computer. By balding I mean it's obvious—obvious to everyone except Doctor Daneeka here. The remaining hair has been spread out on top, but that does nothing to hide the balding pate, and a swift wind almost threatens to rip all of it away.

'Well, I'm afraid, Arthur, that we're going to have to get you booked in for some biopsies.'

Normally this would be the point where I would have the rigmarole of having to arrange biopsies to be taken by a tired, overworked NHS doctor. But I have money, so I am reliably informed that my biopsies can be taken before the end of play tomorrow . . . and before I know it, I am on the move.

So, death could now be coming for me, which is only fair when you think about it. I do clean up the dark souls (with the occasional exception), but surely someone has to clean me up at some point. Aside from my many mental maladies, I have lived exceptionally well (even in France, I read and hunted), and I can have no real complaints. If this is the end, I shall face it nobly.

But I have a daughter now, and I ought to tell her—as inconvenient as it is. But I don't want to. I don't want to tell anyone. Everyone seemed to be rather happy to have me back in their lives and informing them that I may well be about to take a short walk down a dark path is rather unfair. Day one has been thoroughly exhausting, and I take my leave and head towards my flat to get a good night's sleep.

Day two: Day two started terribly! I made the mistake of leaving my work alarm clocks on, and as a result, I was awoken at the crack of dawn. I managed to get back to sleep for a while, but it's never really quite the same, is it?

And since I have most of the day to kill, I may as well, well, kill.

Alan has far outstayed his welcome in this town, never mind this planet, and something needs to be done about it. The urchin played his hand by inserting him into a police investigation—thinking himself safe. But I am tired of charlatans who seem to think I will dance for them. Killing isn't something I do for fun, and Alan is about to find that out the unfun way.

I have Alan's mobile number, so I shoot him a text:

Wanna meet for lunch and talk?

It's pithy, I'll give it that. But I have no real time for niceties when it comes to Alan. The man is a parasite, a tumour, a ticking time bomb . . .

. . . As am I potentially. I shelve thoughts of my potential impending demise and ready myself for lunch. It will be fine. I will be fine.

Alan finally replies two hours later (just in time for lunch) and agrees to meet me at West Quay food court.

And seriously? What is with people and that place? It's bad enough that he works there. I'd want to spend my lunchtime millions of miles away from there.

With clothes on my back and a craft knife in my pocket (what? It might come in handy), I shuffle out to the car and prepare to drive myself into town.

It's 12.08 p.m., Alan said he would be here at twelve, and he is late. It's bad enough that I have had to smell this man's urine up close. To think that he is now keeping me waiting is a step too far. I put my hand in my pocket and wrap it around the small craft knife that resides there. I push the blade out and retract it with my thumb in one swift movement. Then I repeat it again, and again, and again.

In and out.

In and out.

Breathe, Arthur, breathe.

I slide into my head and think about my last sojourn into West Quay. I ended up lingerie shopping with Nigel, and fuck am I glad he's dead. I don't know how my life keeps getting littered with demented pests and I hope that no one comes along to take Alan's place.

I wait.

I wait.

I wait.

I'll be honest; the waiting time is quite helpful. I have no plan. I've invited Alan out for lunch, and that's as far as I have gotten.

Alan is a problem, especially because of his involvement as a police witness. But given that my time here on Earth might be limited, I'm not sure I care. The man is a menace. He is a danger to anyone, including my daughter, and something has to be done about him.

Alan arrives . . . late . . . not only that, but he arrives with a woman called Jenna—and food. Jenna is his girlfriend— and is everyone in love but me?—Jenna and Alan sit, and suddenly, this is awkward as fuck! I was never blessed with tremendous social grace as it is, and now here I am having to entertain Alan and his girlfriend Jenna. How Alan ever got a girlfriend is beyond me, and yet, here I am. I stare at Jenna, she is not what you'd call attractive, but she is a step up on Alan. Alan has only gone and brought her to his place of work for lunch. There is tasteless, and then there is this, and Alan has to go. I let loose my grip on the blade in my pocket and let it fall to the dark recesses of my trousers. To say I had no plan at all would be an understatement. I had thought about opening up Alan in the stalls in the toilet and just pinning this on the Hampshire Hacker. But the girlfriend is an issue, and I'm sure she will notice him missing when he doesn't come back from the toilet.

Now, I am just out to lunch with my new friend Alan and his girlfriend, and I don't even know how to start this conversation.

Fortunately, Alan opens his mouth and starts talking; unfortunately, he immediately starts talking about work. My hand, which is still in my pocket, tenses up. Before I know it, I am fondling the knife again, and the only thing worse than having an unhinged killer insert themselves into your life is having a boring, unhinged killer insert themselves into your life. I hear some insipid talk about Harry Ramsdens, and I turn to Jenna, who has yet to say a word, and I ask:

'So, how did you two meet?'

The insufferable pair's eyes meet, and they stare at each other longingly. Then Jenna turns back to me and says:

'We met on Tinder. Alan here took me out for dinner, and it was love at first sight.'

I look at the pair and consider that they are, in fact, well-suited. One thing is for sure: Tinder is dead to me now, too.

How two people like this can find love is beyond me . . . and I wonder . . . I wonder if Jenna knows. I wonder if she knows what Alan is. Does she know the peril she is in? Does she know she is having lunch with two murderers?

I sit back in my chair and look around the crowded food court. I watch people as they eat and talk, and I wonder how many other people are having lunch with two lunatics.

I'm not a lunatic, am I?

Having accepted that I am here for the long haul and that there will be no murder, it dawns on me that I am starved almost to death. I raise myself from my sticky plastic chair and make my way towards the till. I wander over and stand in line, but before I know what is happening, a hand appears from nowhere and grabs me on the shoulder. I brace myself before I reach into my pocket once more and slide the small knife out of its sheath; I am prepared to remove it when I hear Alan's voice in my ear.

'Here, use my discount card!'

I turn about and find Alan in my personal space. His hand is outstretched expectantly, and in it resides a small red card. I take it from him, and he departs back towards the tables. He stops and turns on his way back towards Jenna and says: 'Get the fish and chips!'

My fish and chips arrive, and I immediately tuck in—anything to save myself from this riveting conversation. I tuck some fish into my mouth, which is, admittedly, very good, and I ruminate as I chew.

This is day two of my two weeks. It is not exactly how I expected that I would be spending my time. I have twelve days until my daughter finds out just what a monster I am, and here I am, spending my time eating lunch with one of Hampshire's most wanted. The fact that I am probably top of that list notwithstanding. I wonder (again) how many other people are unwittingly having lunch with a lunatic. Is it just Jenna? Am I the only one in Hell?

I finish my mouthful and then consider that it is probably better to make the best of a bad situation. Before I have a chance to regret my actions, I open my mouth to speak.

'So, what now?' I ask both Alan and myself. Alan doesn't finish what's in his mouth before he opens it, and I am faced with a face full of mushy peas. He looks me dead in the eye and says:

'Jenna and I were thinking of taking a walk in the New Forest; wanna come?'

Ah, the New Forest, Hampshire's beauty spot, and it is beautiful. The problem is, it's not exactly close to West Quay; it is at least a half-hour drive, and that's not including the fact that my last foray into the forest resulted in my ex-wife, Melissa, getting blown apart by a bag of dodgy grenades. That aside, I do like the forest, but I hadn't planned on going there with Alan and Jenna and as I acquiesce, my head is filled with insidious thoughts.

Should I dispatch them both? Are they in on this together? Are they taking me out there to kill me? It would be a peaceful place to free myself of them both, but Jenna, as far as I'm aware, is an innocent victim of all of this.

Alan offers to drive, and the next thing I know, I am in the back of his Vauxhall Corsa—again, what's with people and the Corsa? I might be a bit of a car snob, but I think you can tell a lot about a man by his choice of car. To me, Alan's Vauxhall screams: I am a massive tool, and I am not impressed at being crammed in the back. To make matters worse, Jenna decided to ride in the back with me, and now I'm pretty sure she knows about Alan.

Does she?

'So, I ear you work for the police?' says Jenna. I stare at her dimply face and then out of the window; we are still in Southampton, and time will pass by much more quickly if we fill it with conversation and not awkward fucking silence. The problem is that Jenna doesn't exactly inspire me, and I would rather talk to an angry ape.

'Yes,' I reply.

'Did you know that man? You know, the one wot was killed?'

I nod my head solemnly and bite at my lip. I catch sight of Alan's glare in the rearview mirror, and our eyes entwine. I cannot work out what is going on, and I don't know what to do. I could be being led to my death, like a lamb to the slaughter. I could be about to take the world's most awkward trip to the New Forest. I don't know. My inner demon wants Alan dead, and my reverie has lasted longer than it should have.

'Yes, very sad,' I reply. Then I add, 'But we'll catch them.' Jenna nods and crosses her chest while looking up to the sky. I think it is a religious gesture, but it looks all wrong. Anyway, I am far from an expert on the matter of all things non-secular. And I do my best to move the conversation along.

'So, what do you do for work?'

'Air,' replies Jenna. 'I cut air.'

I assume that she cuts hair and can't slice through the atmosphere. Although, it would be nice if someone could slice through the atmosphere in this car right now. Alan has been suspiciously quiet—short of a better plan, I decide to ask them what they do for fun.

'Walk,' says Jenna, who is now doing all the talking. 'We like to go for walks. It clears the ed.'

I wonder what she has going on in her head that needs clearing, but I don't ask.

We pull up in a clearing, and all of us disembark. It is late April, things are warming up, and there is a general feeling of optimism in the air.

For nature, anyway. I am not feeling at all optimistic about life, for once I have rid myself of these lunatics, I am on a fast countdown to misery.

But it would seem that, for all intents and purposes, Alan and Jenna have brought me here for just that: a walk. Jenna bolts from the car and runs off towards the water; Alan stays and admires a herd of local wild horses. Their attention is not on me at all, and good god, surely, they don't see me as a friend. They should be terrified of being alone in the forest with me, yet here they are, petting horses.

I decide to make the best of a bad situation, and I join Jenna down by the lake. As I arrive, she turns to me and simpers.

'Don't worry,' she says. 'We won't tell nobody about you and that policeman.'

'He was a pathologist—' I begin before I realise that I am wasting my time. So, I thank her before I consider that the only reason I killed Nigel (yes, he was very annoying) was because he wanted me to kill her boyfriend by chopping off his head while he was still alive. I don't add that, however. Nor am I sure that it will be comprehended. One thing is for sure, though. Jenna knows all about Alan. The pair have to go. With Alan still preoccupied with the horses, I remove the small craft blade from my pocket. I walk up behind Alan, check that the coast is clear, and then shuffle to within an inch of him. He clocks me when I arrive, and I say: 'I should have killed you on that bridge!' He doesn't have time to register what has been said before I move the knife up to his neck and open it up straight across. The knife cuts so deep that for a second, no blood flows out. Until finally, the damn bursts and bright red blood billows from his neck and onto the floor.

Suddenly, I hear a shriek from behind me. Jenna is no longer looking at the water but is now staring at me in horror. Between Jenna screaming and Alan dying on the floor, a lot is going on, not to mention a lot of noise. Jenna is screaming, and Alan is gurgling away. It sounds like a weird suction hose, and all of it is too much for my fractured state of mind. I spy the keys to the Corsa, which are still in the ignition, and I jump in and start the engine. Jenna is still bawling down near the water's edge, and I put the car into first and rev the engine hard. The car takes off at a medium pace and lurches down the bank. Jenna gets stuck. Caught like a deer in headlights, and she is rooted to the spot. I drive the car at her, with my fingers wrapped so tightly around the steering wheel that I fear my knuckles may pop. Jenna gets closer and closer and closer, and just when I think she might join me in the car—terminus. The car hits Jenna, who shrieks once more as she is thrown out into the middle of the water. Her body hits the water with a satisfying splash and then begins to sink away from the surface.

Fortunately, the sub-standard safety devices on the car didn't deploy, and no airbag hit me in the face.

I put the car in reverse and quickly depart the scene. I ought to leave it here and burn it, but getting back from the New Forest to Southampton is no mean feat. The car still works, albeit a bit scuffed. So, I set about my return journey to Southampton. And goddammit, what is with people and spoiling the New Forest for me? Last time, it was armed mercenaries; this time, it's a budget version of Mickey and Mallory Knox.

I hit the main road and fall into my head. So much for day two. But at least Alan and Jenna are dead; there is one less problem for me and two fewer sociopaths for the world to deal with.

Day three: I wake up to some mild stiffness in the neck area. It might just have been Jenna, but it was still an impact, and I guess it's unlikely that I can claim compensation.

After returning to Southampton, I took the car down to an abandoned industrial estate, wiped it clean and then set fire to it. Then I walked home, which is a lot of effort given Southampton's capable public transport network. Regardless, walk I did, and then I got straight into my car and headed to the hospital to have my biopsies taken.

And now I can't help but feel a little bit better about things. Granted, I did kill two insufferable pests last night. But if Jenna could accept Alan for who he was, then maybe Olivia will take me for what I am. After all, I do only kill bad people. I know it is a little extreme, but some people do not deserve their place on this planet. I may soon be one of them. Which reminds me, there is the small matter of my time left on Earth . . . time that might be running out. A day has passed since I was biopsied, and there will be results for me to collect soon.

I shelve notions of my mortality and walk towards my closet. I showered last night (burning cars stink) and so I dress and ready myself for a day at work with my daughter.

I sit across the desk from Olivia as I watch her work. She is so much like her mother, and it is unbelievable. As I watch her shuffle papers about her desk, I wonder. I wonder how she will feel when she finds out. I mean, it is better if it comes from me. Maybe she'll see me as Arrow or, better yet, Batman. Just cleaning up Southampton one murderer at a time. Perhaps she'll be proud. Understanding . . .

'No, this one's not for us,' she says as she tosses a file in my direction. My reverie is disturbed by a small manilla file hurtling in my direction, and I react just quick enough to catch it.

'What is it? I manage.

'The boys in blue said it was a double murder,' she murmurs, 'but there is only one dead body. She's not ours until she's dead!'

I look at the brown cover of the file, and I quiver. Could it be? It can't, surely? I've been here before with Nicky, and I swear to God, if Jenna isn't dead, then I really should just be retiring right now. I paw at the top sheet of the file tentatively and look at the inner sheet. Jenna Proctor, 32, in a coma . . . in a fucking coma? What part of being hit by a car into a lake did she not understand? Die! That was your one objective, Jenna.

Okay, so now things are problematic. Jenna is not dead, but I might soon be. I am still wrestling with my decision whether or not to tell my daughter (the policewoman) that I'm a fucking serial murderer. On top of that, I have created a mess of dead bodies lately, and it won't be long before some evidence of my malfeasance turns up somewhere.

The problem with Jenna (unlike Nicky) is that I know for a fact that she is in protective custody, which makes it very unlikely that I will be able to sneak in and finish her off. If she wakes from her coma, there is no telling what she might say, and for the first time in a long time, I don't have a clue what to do. I am starting to regret returning from France, and perhaps I should have stayed in the cold. The clock is ticking—very loudly—and I have eleven days until my daughter finds out that I am the Hampshire Hacker, and I ought to tell her. But how does one even have that conversation? *Oh, hey, sweetie, sit down, and I'll tell you about the time I killed a lawyer in the men's room at a party* . . .

No, it doesn't work like that, and I worry that I'll never have the courage to tell her. I like the way that she looks at me; there is a deference in her eyes, and I never want that to change. As much as I want to tell her the truth, I can't deal with changing her opinion of me, which I will, won't I?

I close the manilla folder. I go to speak, but I think better of it. Then I stand, awkwardly shuffle, clear my throat and say: 'Hey, sweetie, are you all right if I take lunch early?'

I look at the clock on my desk, and it tells me that it is ten a.m.; Olivia looks at it too and then says:

'Sure, Dad, everything okay?'

I nod, and short of a better plan, I turn about and depart. Time to get those biopsy results . . .

I sit in a small sterile plastic chair, and I am sweating. The wait has been just over ten minutes, but it has been a long ten minutes. On the other side of the door, Doctor Daneeka has the results from my biopsy, and I am dying (possibly) to know what they say. Part of me hopes I've got less than eleven days to live, and then I can skip out on all of this bullshit early. The other half of me wants to live. I've nearly been killed—twice—and it's not pleasant. I want to live on. I want to carry on doing the things I enjoy, and death would rather get in the way of that.

The door opens, and I step inside . . .

Okay, so it's not the end of the world. It's just the end of mine. Probably.

I have stage four lung cancer, and my survival rate is about seven per cent, which isn't great. I honestly can't believe it, and yet, believe it or not, it's happening. I can ignore it as much as I want, but it isn't going to stop the tumour on my chest from blossoming into a big bad monster. If there is good news, I might only have weeks to live, and maybe I will be spared the ignoble end, which is my daughter finding out that her father is a monster. Regardless, she will find out anyway and I'd rather those words came from me.

I am nonplussed. I know I am advancing in years, and I know I have smoked heavily most of my life. But this sort of thing happens to other people. Not me.

I have two choices—ostensibly. I can either wait it out and slide away like a receding tide, or I can opt for some very aggressive chemotherapy that is only likely to add a few weeks—maybe months—to my time here on earth. This isn't the turn that I thought my life was about to take, and it puts the rest of these two weeks into perspective.

I leave the surgery, and I am almost maudlin by the time I reach the car. I start the engine and slide into my head. The end of Arthur's reign is looming, and I don't know what I'm supposed to do next.

No one likes bad news, and I have to be the bearer of said news, which doesn't sound like fun. I agree to keep this to myself until I have figured out the rest of the itinerary for the next two weeks. I drive home, enter the house, and go to bed.

Day four: I wake up feeling excessively maudlin. It has been some time since I have been this depressed, but life has a way of shovelling it all on at once.

And I always thought that when death came, it would be sudden. Why do I have to know? Why can't it just take me out at night or in a dark alleyway? Why do I have to wait for the insidious footsteps of death to sneak up on me? Regardless, death is coming for me, and I guess there isn't much for me to do other than enjoy the time I have left. There are (as far as I'm aware) no more Hampshire Hackers out there, so the police trail will go cold. I've had my fill of murder lately, and I've seen all of my friends. But I am lonely. I could very much use the company of a woman . . .

Dating used to be easy. Don't ask me how, but pre-Internet and smartphones, we just managed to make it work . . .

. . . But it would seem that all of that has changed. My friends are all content in their relationships, and we are all way past trawling nightclubs at one a.m. (was that ever a good idea?). They don't have any single, eligible friends. My daughter's friends are all far too young. And outside of people from work, I don't know anyone. There is only one person on this planet who might be able to help me. And good, God, how does this keep happening?

Judy!

Judy has been single for some time now but seems to have a steady stream of one-off love affairs. And I have no idea how she manages it . . .

'Yes, Arthur, what do you want?'

I sit in my armchair at home and stare at the wall. I've heard Judy's words cascade from the earpiece, and I'm stuck.

'Arthur?'

'Yes, Jude.'

'What do you want?'

'Well, I—'

'Spit it out, Arthur.'

'Dating?'

'What about it?'

'How do you do it?'

'I don't, Arthur.'

'But . . . you have me—'

'My God, Arthur, don't tell me you haven't heard of online dating?'

I shake my head. I can't think of much worse.

Judy runs me through the basics and then abruptly hangs up. It's safe to say she didn't appreciate a call at nine a.m. to ask how she gets men. Regardless, I am now armed with the names of several apps, and I turn to my computer and get to typing.

Okay, so this is an issue. Dating apps require photos and a description. Photos I can probably manage. But how the fuck does one even go about describing themselves? Firstly, what kind of self-propagating arsehole do you need to be to be apt at selling yourself? Second, I'm not sure I want to 'sell' myself. And third, what do I even say about myself without just describing a picture of me?

Arthur, 63, once widowed. Interests include reading and murder. All the women in my life have died, and now that I am dying, too, I am looking for love again.

I mean, granted, in this day and age, it might get some takers. But still, as much as I would love to muddle through this on my own, there is only one person young and tech-savvy enough to guide me through this.

Olivia!

I head into the police station only to be told that Olivia is out at a crime scene, so I get back in the car and take a drive.

When I arrive, I know where I am instantly. This was the spot where Nigel met his untimely demise. And I am not overly keen to be back here. But I do have questions about Bumble, so I persevere. I park the Alfa in the questionable parking area and then take the short walk through the brush towards the bridge. I approach from the rear, and I spot my daughter standing on the bridge, looking down at any approaching trains.

'Don't jump,' I say as I arrive. Olivia spins about as if on a sixpence and smiles as I approach. Her grin lasts until I arrive, and her face takes the form of sad contrition.

'Nigel lost his life here,' she says.

I want to roll my eyes, and technically, Nigel lost his life about a hundred yards away in some brush. I don't like that my daughter is back here; I did a poor job of cleaning up, and if they extend the search perimeter, they will find Nigel's blood.

I saunter my way over to Olivia and stand next to her on the bridge. I go to open my mouth to speak, but I realise that pressing her for information about Bumble at a time like this might be deemed insensitive.

'Jenna Proctor was the girlfriend of our witness, Alan,' says Olivia.

'Hmmm,' is all I have to add.

'Something is way off here, Dad. We've had a spate of recent killings, but something doesn't add up. Why go to the lengths of mutilating the bodies only to give that up?'

'Maybe they were interrupted?'

Olivia nods and considers the thought. A train rattles away in the distance, and I remember the sound that Nigel's body made when it was dissected by a train. There is so much rattling about in my head, and admitting that I killed Nigel seems like a very difficult thing to do. Confessing that I killed Alan or ran over Jenna seems like an impossible task, and yet, I have to. Lest Nigel does . . . from the grave. There is also the small matter of my potential impending death and the fact that I need assistance with my online dating profile.

Olivia turns to me and smiles, 'Was there something you wanted, Dad?'

I shake away the notion that right here would make for an interesting shot for a profile photo and shake my head.

'No, I just thought I would see if you needed any help out here?'

Olivia nods. 'Thanks, Dad; I have some boys in blue on their way. We are going to extend the search perimeter; you're welcome to stick about and help if you like?'

Excellent, an extended search. Just what I need . . .

TWENTY-ONE.

Day five: The search perimeter was extended, and Nigel's blood was found. Which is not what I need. Regardless of Nigel's posthumous demands, it would seem that I am starting to stick my foot in it. To make matters worse, my time on Earth (incarcerated or otherwise) may well be coming to an end soon, and I still haven't sorted out June.

June was my ex-nosy neighbour. She would argue, for all to see, with her husband Mike every weekend. It was annoying. It was mildly amusing. Anyway, Mike died, and June went wildly off-kilter. I think June might have figured out what I am . . . but she was in some state . . . then she shot me and ended up in jail, where she's been for twenty-five years. And as angry as I am at having been shot, I really ought to do something about the fact that I am not dead, given that she was sent to jail for my murder.

And since my mind is awash with what might or might not be about to happen, I figure I will do something that I can control: collect June.

Now, there has been a bit of work behind the scenes, but it's all very dull. The thick of it is today is June's release day, and I am on my way to pick her up.

June wound up in HM Prison Bronzefield, which is slightly further from home than I had anticipated on driving, given that it is on the outskirts of London and will involve me having to tackle the M25. So, I put my head down and settle in for the drive . . .

Ring. Ring.

My phone, which is connected to the car's dodgy in-built Bluetooth system, begins to ring. I peel my eyes from the windscreen and drag them across to the centre console.

Judy!

Judy is calling me, which is a problem in itself; talking to Judy is not top of my list of things to do. But, since there is nothing to do when you are trapped in a vacancy, I tap the button and accept the incoming call from my fiendish sister.

'Hullo,' says Judy.

'Hey, Jude,' I reply.

'Where are you going?' she asks as if she can sense I am on my way somewhere important.

'To pick up June.'

'Is that a good idea?'

'It's got to be done, Judy.'

'But June might know—'

'What do you want?'

'Well, fine,' says Judy. 'I won't tell you about Nigel.'

'Judy,' I say, 'stop being gnomic. Spit it out.'

'I've been digging into your friend Nigel . . .'

'Yes, I got that,' I reply. 'He's dead.'

'Arthur?'

'What? He died. He got hit by a train . . . ostensibly.'

'Uh huh.'

'What did you find out?'

'Well, I didn't know that he was dead. I didn't find out much about him other than the fact that he has, well had, a storage unit in Southampton.'

'Where?'

'In Southampton.'

'Yes, but specifically, Judy. There is more than one storage place.'

'Really?'

'Yes.'

'Okay, fine, let me . . . '

The noise on the other end of the phone gets rather 'shuffley' as Judy rummages about with what I presume is an F5 tornado. Then the phone goes quiet momentarily before Judy's non-dulcet tones reappear.

'Erm, the place is called Access.'

'Thanks, Judy,' I say almost sincerely.

'Arthur, what will you—'

'Thanks, Jude. Driving. Gotta go.'

I don't let Judy finish her sentence before I press the 'end call' button. The fact that Nigel had a self-store might just shed some light on what he has on me and where. This is some good news, but it doesn't change the fact that I'm dying. I fall back into my head and carry on the drive to Ashford (not in Kent).

The rest of the drive was as shit as it sounded. There was a rather predictable queue near Heathrow Airport, and since I was on my own, I wasn't able to look at Flight Radar to see what planes were incoming/outgoing . . . which is no fun. The scenery blended together after that, and now I find myself staring at the outside of HMP Bronzefield.

The site was once a school, which is very apropos given the current state of the schooling system. I dare not go inside, lest I never come out. So, I wait outside, propped against the bonnet of my shiny red Alfa. A thought rustles through my brain, and I think that I might be nervous. It has been twenty-five years since I last saw June, and during our last encounter, she was armed with a shotgun. I spent twenty-five years in exile, but I don't know how she will have fared after twenty-five in incarceration. I have no idea whether she will be happy to see me, but picking her up is the least I could do. Most of her family and friends will have had to move on with the notion of her as a murderer, and perhaps I really should pick her brain.

My reverie is interrupted by the gates opening, and a short, slim woman walks out of them.

It's June.

June walks across the road towards me, and I cannot tell what her facial expressions convey. Her hair has been cut so short that it is basically a buzz cut; prison clearly saw her take up smoking, and the lines of her face have been exacerbated by twenty-five years of cigarette smoke and, probably, a lack of moisturiser. Her sentence has been cut short by the fact that I am alive, but she did almost kill me, so there will be no exoneration for her . . .

. . . June saunters slowly up to me, stops and says, 'Hello, Arthur.'

'Hi, June,' I reply, looking her up and down as she stands before me. She is still attractive, and I'll give her that, although the short hair has given her a different complexion. Her clothes fit well, and clearly, June took up exercising in jail. She looks good for someone who has been in the can for twenty-five years.

'Sorry I shot you,' she says as I open the car door for her.

'It's okay,' I reply. 'I survived.' She nods and ducks her head to get into the car. I shut the door and then walk around the far side to mine.

After getting in the car, I start the engine, and then we just sit there in stunted silence as the V6 burbles away in the background.

Silence.

More silence.

I put the car into gear and then set off. I go to open my mouth, but then June speaks.

'You didn't kill Mike, did you?'

I shake my head.

'No,' I say. 'Mike died being Mike.'

June nods.

'But you are a killer?'

Short of a better plan, I nod.

Silence falls in the car again, and I don't quite understand. June knows. June knows that I know, and yet, we are just sitting in a car as it lurches slowly forward.

'So, where to?'

June shrugs: 'I have no idea! My whole life collapsed overnight. I have nowhere to go. Mike's dead. My friends and family abandoned me, and the house was sold.'

'I'm dying,' I say as I turn slowly to June.

She places her hand on my leg, and I hadn't expected the car journey to be this maudlin.

'I'm sorry,' she says. 'For everything.'

'Don't be,' I reply.

'No, really, whatever you are, whatever you do. It's no business of mine. I shouldn't have shot you. I was strung out, in grief, and depressed. For what it's worth, I've always liked you, Arthur.'

My eyes meet June's, and I should be watching the road. There is a shimmer in her eye that, I think, matches mine. I drag my eyes away from hers and turn them back towards the road. And short of a better plan, I head in the direction of my house . . .

Day six: I wake up fresh in the knowledge that Nigel has a self-storage unit and go to leap out of bed. I have to move June's sleeping arm, and I sneak stealthily to the bathroom. We drove on in silence, not saying another word until we got back to mine. June knew where we were going, and the tension didn't break until after we had removed each other's clothes. We made it as far as the sofa before we collapsed in a sweaty heap, and she moaned as my hands made contact with her skin. I entered her and we saw out the rest of the night in each other. I don't really know how or why it happened, but it did, and only after did we speak again. We talked the sun into rising and only fell asleep when it was fully up. I'll be honest, I am fucking shattered, but it was truly wonderful spending the night with someone who saw the real me.

June!

What the actual fuck?

But it does solve the loneliness, and I am now safe in the knowledge that I am unlikely to need dating apps anymore, which is a huge relief.

I leave June asleep in my bed and trudge out to the car. It is just after nine a.m., and the traffic will be vile because we all have to go to the same places at the same time every day. But I persevere.

Thanks to the traffic, it takes me a good forty minutes to get to Access Self-Storage. Judy has sent me all the details, so I walk in like I belong (wearing a hat to deceive CCTV) and go in search of locker number 304.

As I walk, I consider that I hadn't seen this coming. When I returned from exile, I had one thing on my mind and one thing only: my daughter. Never in a million years did I think that I would be shacking up with June or chasing after the ghost of a dead lunatic. I've been up to my ears with killers since I returned, and I have recently hooked up with the woman who was sentenced for my murder (later downgraded to attempted murder). Still, I suppose it is very apposite and totally in keeping with the shit show that has been my life. I wonder if there is a grand plan (did someone plan me?), and

I am deep in my reverie when I stop outside locker number 304.

I came prepared, and I whack the crowbar out from within my sleeve, take a good look around, and then shove the crowbar into the small lock and heave. The lock breaks on the first attempt, and I open the door cautiously and step inside.

At first glance, this is weird. Nigel kept souvenirs, and this is certainly enough to condemn him. I'm not all that happy that I've been to the scene, but I'm here now. There isn't much I can do. I shouldn't be surprised that Nigel liked his keepsakes; after all, he displayed all the classic signs of being a psycho. I look at the collection of belongings before me and take a step back. Certainly, this is enough to get the police looking at Nigel in a very suspicious light, but I cannot touch anything. As much as I want to. Plus, if I had a heart, it would be breaking at the sight. Nigel's version of vigilante justice cannot be trusted, and I need to get out of here. I shuffle downstairs, purchase a replacement lock from the lobby's vending machine and then refasten the place. I make it back to the car before I dip into my head again, and I scratch at it as I sit. I think hope was driving me more than anything. And the reality is, I have no idea how Nigel plans to let my daughter know who I am. I am powerless to stop it, and will people look at me like that? Will I be assessed, judged, and analysed? The somewhat sobering thoughts drift into my head, and I set about heading home. Day six ends on a rather sour note.

Day seven: June was still at mine when I got home, and we talked the evening into submission. It's hard to think of her as the woman who I watched having all those arguments with her husband all those years ago as she sits, topless, at the foot of my bed. I don't know what it is that we're doing, but she needs someone just as much as I do . . .

I left June alone at my house and got in the car. I told her I had plans—which is a lie—and I got in and set off for a drive. It took me forty-five minutes to find a pay phone, and when I did, I called in Nigel's storage unit—anonymously, of course. Fingering Nigel as the Hampshire Hacker won't help my cause, but it will take some heat off some open murders, and it will be exactly what he deserves. The fact that anyone still treats Nigel with any deference is very annoying. Nigel was a bad Hampshire Hacker. And he somehow managed to drag Alan into my life.

I put down the payphone and then take the scenic route back to my car. It's hard to be anonymous these days, but one has to try.

Once back at the car, I rack my seat back on its runners and light up a cigarette. I have a week until my daughter learns the truth about me, and I've barely seen her. Having June in my life (weird) has been a blessing, but what I need is to see my friend. Despite not knowing exactly what I am, sometimes all you need is to be in the company of someone you can trust with all your heart.

'Call Abdul,' I say to the car's inbuilt Bluetooth system.

Much to my delight, the car gets it right the first time, and soon, I am greeted by the dulcet tones of my friend Abdul's voice.

'Hey, Broman Villa,' says Abdul. 'What's up?'

'Hey, Abdul, what are you up to?' I ask.

'I'm just playing golf with Richard.'

'Rich Richard?'

Abdul pauses.

'Yes.'

'Not you, too?'

'Sorry, bros and cons.'

'It's okay,' I add. I know I have been wholly absent since I returned and even more so for the years that preceded that.

'Are you okay?' Abdul asks.

'Yes,' I reply. I think I am. But deep down, I'm probably not. Alan and Nigel have opened my eyes as to what I am, how I'll be considered, and what my legacy will be. I have just one week until my daughter finds out what a monster I am, and despite not wanting to tell her, it will be better if it comes from me.

'It's fine. Go back to golf,' I say.

Abdul and I talk briefly before I hang up. I press my head back into the cool leather of the headrest, and I exhale. Short of a better plan, I drive to my daughter's house, park up and wait. When do I tell her?

Day eight: I had to wait an inordinate amount of time for my daughter to return, and when she did, I spent a good two hours consoling her. Apparently, they found a lot of evidence tying Nigel to some of the crimes committed by the Hampshire Hacker, and she was, almost quite literally, beside herself. As much as I had quite a lot of disdain for Nigel, seeing my daughter so upset was, well, upsetting and I'm even angrier at Nigel than I should be.

The good news—is there ever any good news?—is that Jenna is still in a coma, and I'm hoping she doesn't wake up for a good few weeks. . . or at all.

I'm angry. Nigel was a complete twat, and he has thoroughly fucked up my life. Granted, I killed Matt without any real evidence, but that's not the point. Is it? Am I like them? I shake away notions of stupidity and ready myself for the day. June sleeps soundly away in my bed. Apparently, it's much comfier out of prison.

Once dressed, I walk out to the car and am greeted by a pleasant smattering of sunshine. It is early May, and at least there is one positive.

The situation is: I might be dying, I'm currently sleeping with the woman who tried to murder me, and my daughter, my friends, my family, and everyone ever is about to find out the truth about what I do. I'll be on the national news. It's going to be horrendous. Oh, and Jenna is still alive but not quite kicking.

So, I've decided to do something about all of it . . .

Grace handed me that note at the funeral. Granted, she could have been handing me a blue whale and not even noticed, but maybe that was the point. Jenna knew what Alan was, and both Ophelia and Melissa knew what I was. Who's to say that Grace doesn't know what her husband got up to in his spare time? There is no more grace period.

Since all I have is time, well, I don't. But since all I have is the time I have left, I am happy to wait. If I can put a stop to all this nonsense, then I am happy to spend my days waiting for Grace.

So I am: I follow Grace from her house in Tenby Close to a small nail salon just outside of Southampton. She pulls up, goes in and doesn't come out again. So, I assume Grace works here; it would be a very 'Grace' thing to do.

The day comes and goes in a dull haze as I sit, wait and watch. It is all terribly boring, but Grace does finally reappear at just gone six. And I follow her to a gym on Winchester Road and then to a bar. Grace doesn't seem to be all that upset, but I guess we all grieve in different ways. Grace leaves the bar—finally—and ignores her car. She ambles in the direction of a nearby taxi rank, and now I have my opportunity . . . which doesn't fill me with vim. Yes, I know that kidnapping a drunk woman from a dark street is all a terrible cliché. I know I shouldn't do it. But I need to know what Grace knows. I sneak up behind Grace—she is drunk, so she doesn't notice me—and I give her a swift 'bop' on the back of the head and Grace slumps to the floor. I catch her mid-slump, chuck her over my shoulder and then carry her to the car. Once there, I bundle her into the boot, close it and drive off . . .

Now, I know I said I'm not like the others; I am not some deplorable dickhead out taking advantage of people. I'm not. I'm not. I need to know what Grace knows so that I can get on with my life.

Okay, so we are in an abandoned hotel on the edge of town, and Grace is taped to a chair. I think she is coming to, and I have no real plan. If Grace knows nothing, I have just committed a terrible mistake. Grace will know that there is something wrong with me, and I will be faced with making a horrible decision about Grace's future. On the other hand, if Grace isn't innocent, I will be faced with making a terrible decision about her future. I'm too deep here, but this is all because of Nigel and his malevolent plan.

Grace wakes up and looks me straight in the eye; if there was ever a look that says *I know what you get up to,* that was it. Our eyes meet, and I know that she knows and vice versa. It's like a bad game; I say:

'What is Nigel's plan?'

Grace laughs. It has a wild chill to it, and this girl isn't scared. Grace's laugh passes by me like a ghost; I step closer to her, and I ask her again:

'What's Nigel's plan?'

'You'll never figure it out.'

'What is it?'

Grace leans forward and tests the range of what binds her. The ties stretch as she leans forward.

She laughs again.

'I don't know. I never really knew what Nigel was up to. But that's how it works, doesn't it?' The cadence in Grace's voice is true. She is not making any of this up.

'How much do you know?'

A light from the roof shines off her face, lighting up one side of it. If I were not me, I might be slightly afraid. She wears a formidable smile.

'My husband did what was best for the world,' she says. 'I don't know how he did it, but I know that he did. But you are familiar with this situation, aren't you?'

I take a step back; Nigel and Grace know way too much about my life, and it doesn't make sense. I get the feeling that even if Grace knew what Nigel was up to, she wouldn't tell me. It's fair; I would never have given up Melissa, Ophelia, or even Olivia. I wonder if I have made a mistake; have I played right into Nigel's hands? And now I don't know what to do with Grace. She already knows about me, so if she were going to tell the authorities, she would have done it already. But does she pose a danger to me and my family? How much longer am I going to be around to protect them?

'You can't stop it,' says Grace, who leans as far forward as she can again. The words leave her mouth, and then it is silent. And I'm not sure what I prefer.

'My husband was cleaning up this county. And you stopped him. You're going to Hell, Arthur Norman!'

A small chunk of saliva leaves Grace's mouth and lands on my chin. And the realisation hits me. I cannot leave Grace alive. And before she has a chance to speak again, I remove a knife from the inside of my jacket pocket and ram it into her chest. Grace barely has time to react as the knife enters her heart. It pumps and pumps before its feeble motion stops. Grace slumps back into the chair and her arms go slack at her sides.

It's done.

I take two steps back and let the knife fall to the floor. It lands with a bloody clatter, and I slide off my feet and onto my bum. I clasp my hands against my face and shake my head gently side-to-side.

What have I done? What am I becoming? I've killed so many people since I returned, and I don't know if it's justified. My moral compass is pointing everywhere, and I don't know what's right anymore. But I need to keep my daughter safe; that's what I'm doing . . . right?

I undo the ties that bind Grace to the chair, pick up my knife and remove any trace of me ever being here. The body will be found in time, but for now, it's safe. I have less than a week until Olivia finds out what I am and possibly not many more on this planet.

I amble back to the car, open the door, enter and sit. I rack the chair back on the runners and light up a cigarette, stretching out my long legs. I catch sight of myself in the rear-view mirror, and it is only then that I realise there are tears in my eyes. I start the engine, and I tell myself that only Olivia matters.

Only Olivia matters . . .

Day nine: Time is ticking away.

When I got home, I met June, who was still in my apartment. It seemed that getting out of prison after twenty-five years was an adjustment. We made love until the late hours of the night, and when I woke up, she was gone. A small note said that she would be back later—I hope she is.

Time is not my friend at the moment, and I have no idea if later will even come. And, since I'm getting sentimental in my old age, I decide that it is worth doing the rounds with the people in my life. I have been an absent, friend, brother, and son lately . . . not to mention father. I need to fix that. Starting with my parents . . .

Father's birthday is in June, but I have no idea if I'll make it that long (between incarceration and death, my future is no longer certain), so I make the journey to Kent to see my parents.

The journey should be short, but it is long. Traffic being what it is, it takes me far longer than it should.

But I do arrive, and since Judy is not here, the driveway is free for me to park on.

I pull in and park up. The V6 burbles away interminably, and I give it some revs to liven things up. Ten seconds elapse. Twenty. Finally, my mother's small head pokes itself around the kitchen blind. Movement.

The front door creaks open by the time I arrive, and I open it fully and step inside. My mother greets me with surprise, which is what I was going for.

Surprise, I'm dying and maybe also going to jail for multiple murders!

No, that wasn't quite the surprise I was going for. But it is the sentiment behind it, so I grab my mother and hug her dearly. She returns the gesture, and a cough sneaks out of my lungs. As much as I try to stuff it back in, I can't. The coughing becomes a fit, and my mother lets go of me and trundles off to get some water. She returns with it, and for once, I am grateful for a drink she has given me. The coughing alerts my father, who stops torturing machines, and therefore creating Skynet, and comes to see what all the fuss is about.

'Arthur,' he says, 'what a surprise.'

'Ta-da,' I reply.

Then, as a family, we move into the kitchen, and my mother makes tea.

'To what do we owe this visit?' asks my mother.

'What?' I ask. 'Can't a son visit his parents?'

My father nods and says: 'Well, it's good to see you.'

I'm glad that my appearance is met with some satisfaction. I really should tell them that it might be the last time they see me, but no one likes goodbyes. The afternoon slides into the evening, and before I know it, we are sitting on the deck (it is May), drinking gin and tonics.

'So, what will you do now, Arthur?' asks my mother.

'Well, I'm working for the police, Mum.'

'Yes, but they caught that man, plus, well, you can't do that forever.'

Death, Mum. Death or jail. Or jail then death . . . I think to myself.

'I don't know,' I say. 'I haven't thought about it.' I take a sip of my gin and think about it as I do. Perhaps I should ride off into the sunset. Or rent a boat and sail it into a hurricane? These are all options, but none of them involve my daughter, and that is why I am here.

I stand up and move towards the edge of the deck; at this point, I don't care anymore. I reach into my pocket and grab the packet of cigarettes that resides in there.

'Those things could kill you, you know,' says my mother. I smile the world's most ironic smile and take a deep draw on my cigarette. I consider what I have done. I killed Grace. I don't feel good about it. Yes, she knew, but that would be akin to someone killing Melissa or Ophelia just because they knew about me. For the first time in my life, I honestly don't know if I've done the right thing, and I'm in a real quandary.

'How's your daughter?' my mother asks, changing the subject. I slide back into my head as I consider Olivia discovering the truth about me, and no matter where I turn in my head, I cannot outrun an insidious thought.

'She's fine, busy dealing with dead bodies.' My father baulks at the notion, and my mother looks like I've just offered to slaughter my sister ritualistically. 'What?' I say. 'That's what she does.'

My father shakes his head, and I'd forgotten that we like to pretend that things don't exist in this family. My mind is desperate to leave, but I came here to say goodbye. And since I'm not actually going to say goodbye, the least I can do is try.

'How about a game?' I posit.

I played a mammoth game of Scrabble with my parents. Mammoth, because it does go on. But it goes on even more so when my father insists on taking twenty minutes a turn, only to produce a four-letter word. But he is my father, so we endure. The game ended (finally), and we ate, drank, and talked. And now the parents are fast asleep, tuckered out, tucked up upstairs. I remain awake on the deck, with a blanket wrapped around my shoulders to counter the cool spring breeze. I can feel that the end is coming, and to some extent, I'm fucking relieved. Living life the way I have has not been enjoyable. Never being true to yourself and having to hide parts of yourself away is difficult. And I know, I know, I'm a killer, but I just work with what I have. I didn't ask for this. I didn't ask for any of this.

I finish my cigarette, close the patio doors and step inside. The house is silent as I creep through it and eventually make my way to bed. Tomorrow is day ten.

Sleep.

TWENTY-TWO.

Day ten: I made the mistake last night of arranging a get-together—as part of my farewell tour. It was a mistake. I acknowledge that. But it means I can see Rich Richard, Maureen, and Cathy all at once, which just leaves Judy. I don't think I care if I ever see Judy again. But she is my sister. Needs must. That can wait.

I depart my parents' house and look back through the rear-view mirror fondly. It is an odd place; they are odd people. But it is, no doubt, my last visit, and a small sense of feeling tugs at my sleeve.

But there is no time to dwell.

My journey goes well until I hit the M25, and then time itself seems to slow down. Happily, though, I do emerge on the other side, and before long, I am back in Southampton.

There is so much going on inside old Arthur's brain that I forgot to mention that I gave June a key to my place. So, she has, no doubt, been coming and going. I don't know what June and I are doing, but I very much like having a friend with benefits for the end of the world.

I get home—eventually. Cheers, M25—and I hop into the shower. The gang are meeting me at a Greek restaurant in town, and I slide into my head as water slips down my body. I haven't been to a Greek restaurant since my date with Ophelia—all those years ago. It seems odd to think of her as dead, and I would be raging if I'd thought someone had killed her. Maybe it's the cancer, maybe that has been sent to stop me. Either way, I am feeling terribly maudlin by the time I leave the shower, and I have to paint on a smile as I do my hair.

Tonight will be fun.

Tonight will be fun.

My taxi arrives and I am ready. I get in. I sit. I talk . . . nervously. I don't know why I'm nervous; these are my friends, after all. But, I suppose, this is something of a 'last supper', and there I go comparing myself to Jesus again. I was going to invite June. But inviting the woman who nearly killed you—who you're now sleeping with—seems in bad taste even for me.

The taxi pulls up outside the restaurant, and I step outside. The air is warming up, not enough to make it feel like I'm in Greece, but enough to believe it is not England. And just as I think about turning around and going home, I catch sight of Abdul's face in the window, and it shines out to me as a lighthouse does to a lost sailor. I return his grin and step toward the restaurant door.

'Arthur,' they say as I enter. A cheer rises from my table of friends as they rejoice at my appearance. I sit down, bewildered, I don't feel like a winner, I certainly don't feel like a good guy, and yet, and yet, all these people are so happy to see me.

'Hi, guys,' I say as I sit. I am sitting for all of ten seconds before a young waitress scuttles over to me and takes my drink order. I order a beer and relax as I do. The waitress, who barely looks old enough to be up this late, disappears into the kitchen, and I look at the group assembled in front of me.

'So, how goes the dating, Arthur?' Cathy asks me. And word has spread about my sojourn into the complicated, soul-sucking world of online dating. There are some bad people out there. And that is coming from a world-renowned murderer. My drink appears in front of me, and I take a sip from it and smile.

'It's going.'

'Ooh, what's the dirt?' says Maureen, in that intense way that she does, well, everything.

'It's early days yet,' I say. I figure if I buy myself enough time, I will be dead before I have to admit that I'm fucking June.

Fucking June.

The conversation reaches its nadir, and then the food arrives—enough to feed an army. But I have worked up quite the appetite lately and I am happy to lay waste to as much food as possible.

The evening quite quickly descends into drunken stories, and before I know it, I am on my way home again. Days are all sliding into one another, and it doesn't matter how much time you have, or how hard you try to hold on to it, it will just slip away.

Day eleven: I wake up sporting a sore head, and hangovers at this age are just unfair. Why can't we have something nice? Why does there always have to be a consequence? I sit up slow motion slowly and look around the apartment. I realise that I am on the sofa. I don't fully remember getting home last night, but I have at least managed to unburden myself of my shoes.

I sneak past sleeping June and into the bathroom. I have had two weeks to deal with this, but it does not feel like it. The sand in my timer is running out. And I still ought to see Judy. My disdain for her is great, but she has been quite good to me lately. Driving, hungover, up to London is surely some punishment, and maybe I am in Hell. But Judy needs to be seen. It's weird. I feel as though I can be my real self with Judy, which is something I never thought I would say.

I pack a small bag, write a note for June, and then hop in the car. Judy hates surprises, so at least something good will come of today.

When I arrive at Judy's place in London, she is out. My head is banging like there is a rave in there . . . and I still fucking hate raves. So, I do the sensible thing, and I take myself to a nearby bar to sit and wait for her to get home.

'How's it going?' asks the overtly friendly bartender. I smile and nod and reply that *it's going*. He takes this as a sign that I don't want to talk, and he pours my double whiskey in silence. I don't particularly like whiskey, but it is a nice drink to nurse on the rocks, and it feels like one of those days.

Judy finally appears several hours later, and I am slightly drunk by this point. Judy, as ever, is surprised to see me, and, as per always, I can't tell if she is pleased to see me or is arranging for someone to have me taken down by the Thames and shot.

But she is my sister, and I do need to say my goodbyes . . . as it were.

'What are you doing here, Arthur?' she asks as we ride the elevator up to her penthouse. The music fills the awkward silence, which gives me time to work on my reply.

'Can't a brother just drop in on his sister?'

'They can,' she replies. 'You don't.'

I am mildly offended, granted, whenever I usually see Judy, it is because I am after something. Today, however, I am simply saying goodbye to my sister.

Ding!

The elevator arrives, and we step out into Judy's apartment. I've been here before, but the scene is always breathtaking. The penthouse looks out over the City of

London, but being so high and well insulated, gone are the usual rattles and honks of the city. Instead, it is serene silence, and I am as gobsmacked as ever. Judy moves through the flat like a Queen on a chessboard. She glides passed everything, and before I know it, I have another whiskey on the rocks in my hand. I've drunk too much today, but what's it going to do? Kill me? Incarcerate me?

We sit in the big, comfy armchairs by the window, and I stare at the Thames while Judy prattles on about her day. My mind, as ever, is not where it should be, and I force myself into the fore.

'Arthur?'

'Yes,' I reply.

'How is everything?'

I pause.

I look at Judy.

Her asking me how things are catches me out, and a small tear trickles down the side of my face. It seems like an odd question to catch out a monster like me, but I do feel, and it feels like an eternity since anyone asked me how I am.

How am I?

I'm dying.

I've killed people; I'm not sure they deserved to die.

I'm a monster.

I've only just reconnected with my daughter, and now I'm about to lose her. I'm sleeping with the woman who shot me, and my friends, although still present, moved on in my absence.

And worst of all, no one that I truly cares about knows the truth about me. They will all leave when they find out, and I will die alone.

'I'm okay,' I tell Judy. 'I'm okay.' Judy smiles, and I take a sip of my drink. That's what we say, right? That we're okay, that we're doing fine? I know I'm not exactly normal, but I think I speak for most of us when I say that none of us are any-fucking-where-near fine.

'How are you?'

Judy opens her mouth, but I'm gone again. Maybe I really am a monster . . .

Day 12: The rest of the night with Judy was rather wholesome; we took several trips down memory lane and remembered that we did, in fact, grow up together. It might have been far from a normal childhood, but it was ours, and it is nice to have someone to discuss it with.

I bade Judy goodbye and got back in the car. I got as far as the M3 motorway when the phone rang, and I connected to the call to hear the dulcet tones of my daughter's voice ringing in my ear.

'Dad,' she says. *Dad . . . Dad . . . Dad. I'm a fucking Dad.*

'Yes,' I reply eagerly.

'I'm having a get-together tonight, is there anyone you want to bring?'

'Who's coming?' I ask.

'Abdul, Maureen, Richard and Cathy.'

It's always weird to hear Richard being called just Richard.

'Anyone else?' I ask, more out of fear.

'No, that's why I wanted to ask you.'

I don't have to think for very long to realise that there aren't that many other people in my life . . . apart from June. I realise that I have said that it would be weird to bring the woman who almost killed me to a dinner party, but I am dying, and she is probably the closest person to me at the moment, so I relax my stance.

'Just June,' I reply.

Olivia's reply is a mixture of surprise and concern, but she fields it well, and before I know it, I am back in my own head.

So here I am, walking down memory lane hand-in-hand with June, who is also deep in her past. This was my house; the house next door to it was June's. I used to watch her bicker from the upstairs window of my house. And now that I say it, it sounds weird. The two of us are in tune, and we saunter down the path to my daughter's house. The two of us are late—we were copulating—and everyone will already be in attendance. I am nervous. Me, Arthur, nervous? But, yes, I am. I am rather enjoying having June in my life, but bringing the woman who shot you to dinner is just a tad too much as far as conversation starters go.

I am also aware that I am skating on very thin time. My life is about to culminate in an end that's too depressing to contemplate. I have a mere two days to decide what I want to do. The selfish part of me would abscond; leave before the truth comes out. But that would be selfish, and Arthur Norman is no coward. We reach the door, and I raise my hand to it. My contact with June parts and my fist raps against the hard wood of the door.

Silence.

Then footsteps.

The silence bursts the moment the door opens, and my daughter stands there in all her glory. I see her. I see her and I realise that it has been too long since I last saw her. Coming back to England was for her, and I've been running around on a fool's errand ever since.

'Dad,' she says. I hand her the bottle of wine that I brought, and I step into the house and disrobe. June pauses for a moment, looks around, and then steps into the house. These are my friends; I am pleased to see them, but I would rather be anywhere but here right now.

I usher June into the dining room, and we sit; the hum of the chatter dies and then rises again, and we integrate ourselves into the conversation.

'Arthur,' says Maureen, 'and June?'

June nods and introduces herself to the assembled gang. I would introduce her, but aside from being my neighbour in a past life, I don't know much about her. I sent her to prison—she did shoot me—but I don't even know what she did before that. I am slightly bashful at my lack of knowledge, and I let June take centre stage for a moment. My friends, who care most about my happiness, welcome June with open arms, and it is nice to have people in your life who only care about you. Guilt tugs at my sleeve once more when I remember that I've been deceiving these people for years, and I need to get out of my head.

'Cathy,' I say, 'have you changed your hair?'

She nods, and there is at least one plus point for me for my observational skills. It doesn't quite make up for the fact that in a few days, this will be known as dinner with the Hampshire Hacker, but still . . .

Olivia hands me a plate of sliced meats, and I smile. My hand makes contact with hers, and our eyes meet; she looks so much like her mother; it is unreal.

The evening ploughs on into the night, and before I know it, we are all sitting in the open-plan living room. I sit in an armchair, and June sits on the floor between my legs; despite being May, there is a chill in the air, and I have a blanket draped over my shoulders. The others have gone home, and it is just June, Olivia and me.

'Will you come to work tomorrow, Dad?' Olivia asks. 'I think we have some new evidence in the Hacker case.'

'New evidence?' I ask.

'Yeah, we think we've found the car that was used in the hit and run.'

I nod. I didn't dispose of it all that well. I hope that fire cleansed all of my sins.

'How is she doing, Jenna, is it?' Olivia looks at June and then considers that it is okay.

'She's improving. There is still no prognosis for whether she will come out of a coma or not.'

I nod. It's annoying. Maureen has easy access to Jenna; she could finish her off for good. I wonder, would she, for me? Would anyone? I look at June, on the floor between my legs, and consider that although she hasn't asked, she knows. She knows exactly what I am. I consider that Ophelia knew, Melissa knew, and even Judy knows. If my daughter truly loves me, she will be okay with it, too. Right?

There are too many secrets piling up in my brain. Most of them revolve around death of some sort what I would give just to be normal.

June stirs near my feet, and I can see that she is tired. I slap my knees like all good British people, and this signifies that I have a need to leave. Everyone stands, and we say our goodbyes. Before I know it, we are in a taxi on our way home.

Day 13: Unlucky number thirteen! But it might be my last day as a free man. The last day that my secrets (some of them anyway) stay under wraps.

I stir and I notice that June has gone. She said she was going to spend a few days with her ageing mother, which is probably a good thing. I'd like for everyone to be as far away from me as possible when this all comes out. I stand from the bed and make my way down the small wooden stairs. It's weird; all this time, I have been counting down the days, trying to hang on. But no matter how much you try to hold on to time, it slips through your grasp. The day is almost here. Tomorrow, my daughter finds out who I am. Perhaps I ought to have done more to try and stop it, but Nigel was an organised monster. This is like trying to avoid getting old. It will happen regardless. My only hope is that my daughter will see it the way I do; see me for who I am.

I get into the shower and try to wash away notions of the impending doom. I agreed, last night, to spend the day with my daughter. Just the two of us. No work. No outside influences. So, that is exactly what I'm going to do. I dry off, dress and then step out into the morning. The May sun warms my face, and this is a good day for the zoo. Just a father taking his daughter to the zoo . . . what could go wrong?

I take the small walk across the road and enter the car. The first thing I do is rack the seat back and light a cigarette. I know these small death-filled tubes have probably helped bring about the end of Arthur, but I can no more stop what's happening than I can stop the world from turning. It's best to lean into it. I drag out my cigarette, and when it is finally done, I start the engine and put the car into gear.

I feel numb.

It is do or die today.

Either I tell her now, or Nigel does it tomorrow.

I need to do it. I am Arthur Norman.

But, honestly, how does one even go about saying something like this?

We arrive at the zoo and park. To say it is a zoo is a bit of an overstatement—it's Marwell; if you know, you know. It's not quite a zoo. But, after some mild faff, we get inside and start staring at the animals.

'You all right, Dad,' Olivia asks me.

And no! No, I'm not all-fucking-right. We decided to come to the zoo. The fucking zoo. Here are all these animals locked up in cages, and that is very much how I might be this time tomorrow—locked in a cage. Me, Arthur Norman, locked up. Incarcerated. And it won't be a short sentence; it will be the rest of my fucking life.

So, no. I'm not okay.

'I'm fine,' I say. Because that's what you say.

'You had something you want to talk about, Dad.' The word 'Dad' hits me as I stare at the penguins. They flip and flap about and so does my mind as the word 'Dad' does summersaults in it. Arthur Norman, police consultant, friend, dad, murderer . . .

It's true. I did tell her I have something to talk about. And I said it could wait until later. Apparently now is later, and are we going to talk about this at the zoo?

Honestly, this is one of the worst places I can think of to have the 'discussion'. This is the last place you expect to hear your father's sordid, dark little secrets. But at the same time, I am wracking my brain, and I'm not sure there is a good place to tell your daughter that you're a murderer.

I find a quiet place away from the madding crowd, and I sit us down on a tatty wooden bench. I look into Olivia's eyes, and all I see is her mother. It is haunting, really. And suddenly, I don't feel that bad about this. I look into the eyes of Ophelia and my daughter, and I say:

'Darling, I'm a murderer. I kill bad people.'

'What?'

'I kill people.'

'That's not funny, Dad.' Olivia sweeps a part of her hair behind her ear, and there's that word again.

'Dad.'

What kind of dad does this?

But I am an animal. I am a monster. Maybe I should be locked up like a lion at the zoo. I've killed so many people since I returned, and everyone I know has been put at risk by me. I like to tell myself that I only kill people who deserve it, but I'm kidding myself. The truth is, I'm not the perfect monster that I thought I'd be.

'I'm dying!'

There it is. I've said it out loud again. It's happening. It's real. I look into the tearful eyes of my daughter, and I realise that I'm not ready. I don't want to leave her behind.

'Dad. What?'

'I'm dying.'

Olivia wraps her arms around me and holds me, and holds me, and holds me. She holds me for as long as it takes for her to get it. She holds me, and fuck, I think I'm choking back a tear. This can't be the end.

Olivia removes herself from me, wipes at her beautiful eyes, and says:

'How?'

'Cancer. Lung.'

'How bad?'

'Stage four.'

'Four . . .' the word squeaks from her lips.

I nod.

Olivia places her hands on her hips and goes to speak. Thinks better of it. Then exhales.

'I'm sorry,' I say.

'How long have you known?'

'Not long.'

'Who else knows?'

'You, June, and Doctor Daneeka.'

'Who?'

'He's my doct—'

'Yeah, I got it.'

I nod. She seems angry. She should be angry. Fuck it, I'm furious.

'Well,' she says, turning to me, 'there's chemo, right?' Something?'

I shake my head.

'It's too late.'

'It's never too late.'

'Olivia, I'm a murder—'

'I don't care, Dad. I don't care what you are; you're my father. You can't be dying.'

Olivia starts to shake. And I'm not sure if what I'm saying is landing. I kind of need to know. I don't want her to get information from Nigel tomorrow and have it be a shock. I did tell her. I did. She seems to be taking it rather well.

'Olivia, I'm old. I'm—'

'You're sixty-fucking-three. You're not old, Dad. And you're fighting this, whether you like it or not.'

I nod. I don't know what to say. But I sure have ruined our little trip to the zoo. The animals, that have been shoved in cages, are just begging to be looked at, and here we are, talking about all this morbid nonsense.

A light rain starts to fall from the sky. It lands on Olivia, and I see her shiver. I place my hand on her arm, but she jumps and almost shakes it off.

'Sorry,' she says, 'that was just a lot.'

I nod. I keep nodding. I'm not sure how you follow on from 'I'm dying.' It is quite the non-sequitur and a definite mood killer.

'Let's get you home, shall we?' I say, like all good fathers do.

Olivia nods. At least I'm not the only one nodding.

We stand and make for the exit.

It's been a sombre day.

Day 14: Terminus.

It's here. The day I've been dreading, and I don't know what to do with myself anymore. This countdown has been the only real thing driving me on lately, and now that it's here, I feel, well, a little bit empty.

I dropped Olivia back at hers and left her with a promise that I'd fight this. It was a tense car journey home, and neither of us said anything.

But she knows. I think. And she wants me to live. Maybe she'll come to terms with it. Ophelia did. Maybe she sees the good in what I do.

Maybe.

Maybe.

But the good news is that for the first time in a few weeks, I am off Nigel's hook. There is nothing that he can do to me now.

Well, this information could find its way into the media . . . that could happen. But I don't think that's Nigel's plan. I think he wanted me to squirm. I think he assumed that I'd wind up in trouble.

But none of that is happening. Yes, I squirmed a bit. But that is all in the past now. My daughter knows the truth about me, and clearly, she doesn't care one bit. The weight that is off my shoulders is immense.

Finally, I get out of bed. My body is lighter today, and I almost skip to the bathroom. Once there, I set the shower to a medium temperature, and I wash my soul clean.

I step out of the shower anew, and it looks as though my adventure might continue. I make a note to call the hospital, and I dress.

I struggle into my shorts and the phone rings. I check the ID to see that it is my parents. I could ignore this. I should ignore this. But my good mood prevails, and I pick up the phone on the second ring.

'Hello.'

'Arthur?'

'Yes, Mum.'

'Oh, good, it's you.'

Yes, Mum, it's me. You phoned me, you got me!

'How are you doing, Mum?' I ask.

'I'm okay. The doctor is very happy with my blood tests.'

'That's good to hear, Mum.' I say, wondering to myself what the fuck they were checking her blood for.

'I just spoke to your daughter,' says my mother. 'She sounded upset.'

'Did she say anything?'

'No,' says my mother. 'Just that we should call you.'

'I'm okay, Mum,' I say.

Bleep.

The phone clicks and suddenly I can hear the call of the void as I'm put on speakerphone.

'Hello. Hello, Arthur,' says my father. 'What's going on?'

I sigh.

'Arthur, you still there?' says my mother.

'Yes, Mum, I'm still here.' Although, I wish I wasn't.

'What's happening?' says my father.

'Nothing, Mum, Dad. Nothing is happening.'

'Then why did Olivia tell us to call you?' asks my mother.

'We just had a bad day at the zoo, Mum. That's all. We'll be fine.'

I should tell my parents about my impending doom. I should. But hopefully, if I get chemo, I'll live just long enough that they'll go first, and I won't have to tell them about it.

It's not that I don't want to—it is—but I know they'll just make a lot of undue fuss about it. My parents. They don't get involved unless they get fully involved. Plus, it's not that big a deal. We all die, right?'

'We started watching a new programme last night. What was it called?'

'The Manager of the Night,' says my dad proudly.

'I think it's the Night Manager, Dad,' I reply.

'No, no, I don't think it is,' says my father fervently.

'Okay,' I say. I look at my watch, which tells me that it is just after nine. Realistically, I have absolutely nowhere to be, but they don't need to know that.

'Guys,' I say. 'I'd love to stay and talk. But I have somewhere to be.'

'Okay, well, we'll have to have you down soon,' says my father.

I nod. I agree verbally. We say our goodbyes, and then I hang up. As always, stoicism wins in this family, and we manage another conversation where we don't discuss anything. Safe from my parent's wrath, I smile, grab my keys and then saunter out to the car. It is a lovely spring day, and I have nowhere to be. I hop in the car, adjust my seat to a driving position and then gun the engine. For the first time since I got back, I feel like I am back. It would seem Arthur Norman is treasured, and as a result, I am sticking about for as long as possible.

I manoeuvre the car out of the space and set off in the direction of the New Forest.

A text comes in from my daughter as I drive. I should ignore it. I could ignore it. But curiosity burns deep into my veins, and I pull over (because I'm not a dick) and check my phone.

Hi, Dad. Just to let you know that Jenna didn't make it. Not sure what you're up 2, but do you want to come over later?

Jenna is dead. Thank you, Jenna. That's another loose end that I didn't need hanging over my head. Jenna up and dying is awfully convenient for me, and I thank my lucky stars that she is. I text a reply that indicates I would love to come over, and it's then that I notice a new email, too.

I open the email immediately. I open it because the sender is Nigel Dawson. I open it quickly and read the two words that are contained within it.

Got ya!

Is all it says. Nothing more. Nothing less.

Fair fucking play, Nigel. I am gobsmacked. The whole thing was a fucking wind-up. Nigel got me to admit to my daughter that I am a murderer. Well done, Nigel. I'm not even mad; I'm impressed. I go to reply before I remember that Nigel is dead, and I set my phone back into its cradle and continue on my drive.

The joke is on you, Nigel.

The joke is on you.

TWENTY-THREE.

I'm back!

No, I really am back. I am back at my daughter's house, back where it all started. I am back where I belong, and I am doing what I'm supposed to do.

It's a new chapter for me. I have my friends, my family, June, and my daughter. I will go on new adventures and make new memories. The Hampshire Hacker is dead. That is all in the past, and I am free to move on and kill in silence.

Am I perfect?

No.

But who on this planet is? We all make mistakes, and even the very best of us does something they are not supposed to on occasion. So, I occasionally slip? My intentions are good, and that's all that really matters, right?

I clutch the bottle of wine that's in my hands as I walk down the driveway; I'm nervous, I am. I feel like I now have the opportunity to properly get to know my daughter. I feel like she knows the real me now, and since we've got past that, we can get by with anything.

Cancer be dammed.

You lose. I, Arthur Norman, win.

I am almost skipping as I reach the door. The sun is in the sky, and there is a grin planted firmly on my face. I am in heaven. There is no doubt about it.

I reach the front door and knock. I hear a noise from the inside, and before long, the door swings open, and I can see the beautiful face of my darling daughter. Her eyes well up as they make contact with mine, and she ushers me in.

I follow my daughter into the house and into the living room. I set the wine bottle down on the table and remove my hoodie—it is warm in here. Olivia goes into the kitchen, and

I hear her shout. Go on into the dining room, Dad. Everyone is waiting for you!

Everyone. Is. Waiting. For. Me.

How grand?

The sneaky devil must have arranged a surprise party to celebrate my new start. I catch sight of myself in the mirror atop the fireplace. I arrange my hair, and I realise that for the first time in years, I am smiling. With my hair neatly arranged, I move towards the dining room. The door is closed, but I can already picture Abdul, Maureen, Rich Richard and Cathy on the other side. Maybe my sister is here? Perhaps Aga and Phil. Maybe even some of the offspring.

I reach the door. I place my hand on the handle, and it trembles slightly.

Act surprised, Arthur. Act surprised.

I open the door.

I step inside . . .

. . . 'Arthur Norman, get down on the floor!'

Guns!

Police!

'Arthur Norman, put your hands behind your head and get down on the floor. You are under arrest.'

Fuck!

This isn't the new chapter I had in mind . . .

As an independent author, I thrive on reviews. If you enjoyed the book (or didn't) please, please can you leave a review on Goodreads or Amazon (or both).

ACKNOWLEDGEMENTS:

I would just like to say a big thank you to Jack and Amelia for reading advanced copies of this novel and pointing out all my mistakes.

Thanks to everyone who has liked or shared a post, downloaded a book, or left a review; it all adds up.

And thanks in advance to those who will buy this book as soon as it comes out . . .